# ALLIE SAMBERTS

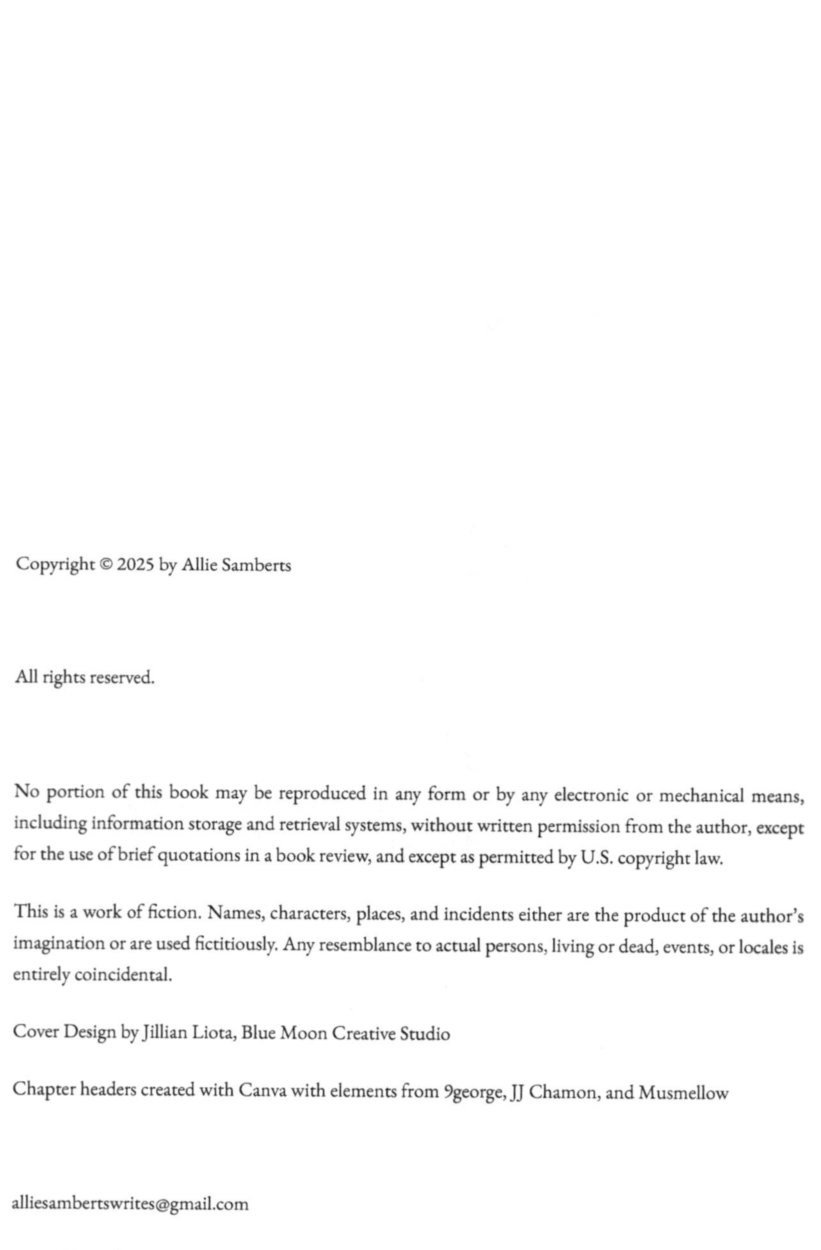

For my dad.

Thanks for all the nutcrackers!

# Author's Note

AT THIS POINT, THE Allie Samberts Chaos Novella is a yearly tradition. Last year, it was *Pumpkin to Talk About*, which started as an exercise in novella writing and also as a way to appease my readers who were feral for Mike. This year, we have *A Holly Jolly Romance*—a quick, adorable, kind of spicy book that started with a story I told my street team that wouldn't get out of my head until I got it on the page.

This book is intended to read like a Christmas movie. The plot is simple, the characters are cute, the small town is full of meddlers, the banter is definitely bantering, and everything is tied up in a nice little Christmas package pretty quickly. If you're looking for a realistic romance novel, you won't find that here. I invite you to suspend your disbelief and enjoy some Christmas magic in these pages.

As with all my books, my main characters are adults. They drink and swear and have on-page, open-door relationships. This one is less spicy than my others, so there's only one open-door scene in the second half of Chapter 12. I believe on-page intimacy is important for character development, but you can do with that information what you will.

There aren't many content warnings to be found in this book, but I know the holidays are a hard time of year for those who are grieving lost loved ones. Lo's

Grams has passed away before the book begins, but she appears in a lot of ways in the book, as does Lo's grief. If that isn't something you can read this holiday season, take care of yourself. The book will be here later if you want it.

Above all, *A Holly Jolly Romance* was so fun for me to write. I needed it. I hope you have fun with it, too.

# Chapter 1

## Lo

"Wʜᴀᴛ ɪɴ ᴛʜᴇ ʜᴏʟʟʏ jolly hell is this?"

I know what it is. It's a nutcracker. Sent in the same green box with the same red ribbon I get every year on December first. But this is not a normal nutcracker. There is no tall, crown-like hat. No candy cane staff in his hand. No joyful red suit.

This nutcracker is carved in a shockingly realistic rendition of Father Christmas, complete with fluffy white hat, wiry white hair and beard, and snowy white coat. But that's where the realism ends. It's stout—about half as tall as the other nutcrackers in my collection. And its mouth is painted bright red, starkly contrasting against the white-painted teeth

This is the stuff of nightmares.

No. Worse. It's a sleep paralysis demon. I can't put this thing on my mantle. It's going to haunt me.

My roommate, Natalia, bounces into the room, her bright red apron covered in flour and sugar. Her black hair has been wound into a messy bun tilted precariously on the top of her head, and her dark eyes are full of mirth as she glances at the box in my hand.

"Is that your nutcracker-of-the-year?" she asks, bounding over to get a better look. I clutch the box to my chest so she can't see it, trying to save her from the horror that lies inside. Literally, it's lying in this box like it's a coffin. Only I realize too late that I don't really want this thing crushed against my chest, either. Shivering, I quickly place it on the entryway table and back away slowly.

"It's really gross this year."

"What do you mean, 'really gross?' It's a nutcracker. How bad can it be?"

"See for yourself." I wave at the box.

Natalia takes a few steps toward it. I stay right where I am. I'm not entirely sure the thing isn't going to jump out at us and start brandishing some kind of knife. Or worse, mistletoe. No way would I put my lips on that thing. I shudder again at the thought.

She bends at the waist and peeks inside. When she gets a good look, she rears back immediately, and some of the flour flakes off her apron and onto the floor.

"That should be illegal." Her nose crinkles up as she winces.

"I can't believe they let it cross state lines."

"I feel like they're getting progressively weirder," Natalia muses. "Wasn't last year's the one that had a music box attached that would play at random intervals even when no one was touching it?"

Shaking my head, I inch closer to the box to snatch the envelope that's sticking up just over the edge. "No, that was the year before. Last year's was in the shape of a teddy bear."

Natalia snaps her fingers. "That's right. It was fuzzy." She shakes her head in disbelief. "Damn, Lo. Where did your grandma find these things?"

"I have no idea," I mutter as I tear open the envelope. The only thing weirder than the nutcrackers themselves is the fact that I keep getting them. December first. Every year.

Every December first for my entire life, my Grams has given me a nutcracker. I have thirty of them in various plastic tubs in our apartment storage unit. Scratch that, there are now thirty-one...if you can call that thing a nutcracker. The way my mom tells it, it started as a joke in the hospital. I was born unexpectedly in a whirlwind delivery just before midnight on November thirtieth during a snowstorm and to a single mother. Grams was supposed to be there to help Mom, but she couldn't get there in time. The only thing the hospital gift shop had that didn't look like pink had thrown up all over it was a nutcracker. So Grams bought it, brought it up to the hospital room, and famously said, "Well, it's no gold, frankincense, or myrrh, but it'll do." And every year since then, on December first, she's given me a new nutcracker.

Even though she passed away four years ago.

Somehow—and no one is really sure how, though we have our suspicions—she has been sending me nutcrackers posthumously. And every year, they come with a note written in her scrawling, perfect cursive.

It's the oddest thing that has ever happened to me, but no matter how much I hate to admit it, I'll be sad when they stop coming. Because they have to eventually. Right?

As I skim this year's letter, my heart squeezes with the knowledge that her gnarled hands touched this paper. Grams was never the sentimental type. She was less of a crochet-you-a-blanket grannie and more of an I-won't-take-any-shit grannie, and I absolutely adored her for it. She was grannie goals when she was alive. When she moved into a nursing home in the city after Gramps died, she was still feisty as hell, even as she started misremembering things toward the end.

And if we're being honest, she's grannie goals even after death. I mean, who has the foresight to continue to send a traditional birthday gift from beyond the grave?

My Grams, that's who.

I can hear deep breathing in my ear, and I catch Natalia leaning over my shoulder to read the letter in my hands.

"Huh," she says. "I always forget your name is Gloria."

"Named for the woman herself," I sing-song as I continue to skim the letter. My mother named me for her mother, which was sweet, but it was mostly because my birthday was so close to Christmas and she thought it would be cute for me to have a Christmas-adjacent name. Cute isn't the word I'd use for it. Not after listening to all of the kids on the playground singing *glooooooo-oo-oo-oo-oo-oooooo-oo-oo-oo-oo-ooooooo-oo-oo-oo-oo-ooooooria* over and over again for the entire month of December.

*In excelsis Deo* my ass.

"Hey, here's your yearly reminder"—Natalia points a flour-covered finger at the middle of the second page—"about the bookshop."

"Oh." I wave her off. "You know she's been trying to get me to check in on the shop space for years."

"Are you going to do it this year?"

"No." Nor will I any year. I haven't been back to Riverbend Springs, Iowa since I graduated high school fourteen years ago, and I don't plan on going back again ever. No matter how much I loved Grams or her shop—The Nook and Granny Bookstore—there isn't anything that could get me to leave Illinois and traipse all the way back over the river and through the woods to my hometown, population 2,890. As soon as I graduated, I left for school in DeKalb, got a job teaching fifth grade in Aurora, and never looked back. Once she was officially an empty-nester, Mom left shortly after me, and when Grams settled into the nursing home, there was especially no reason for me ever to return.

Not now. Not ever. No matter how many creepy nutcrackers she sends to make her point.

"Besides," I say. "I'm not sure why she'd need me to go there. They sold the shop before Gramps died. It's probably a parking lot by now."

Despite my best efforts, the idea of the shop no longer existing sends a pang of sadness through me. It was my favorite place in the entire world. It always smelled like cinnamon and clove, and there were so many books to choose from. When I was a kid, I used to go there every day after school—one of the perks and drawbacks of having a single mom was that Grams took on a lot of my upbringing.

I'd hide among the bookshelves, rearranging the toys and trinkets that were for sale. Sometimes I'd select a book, but usually Grams had a new one waiting for me. I'd take it and cozy up in the beanbag chairs in the back room and lose myself in whatever world awaited me between the pages. My best friend, Liam, would join me, too. Or...former best friend. And when I worked there in high school, he'd show up almost every day to wait for me to close up so we could do whatever it was teenagers did. I can't remember most of it now. It's been so long, and I've put a lot of it out of my memory.

Natalia hums with uncertainty as she pokes at the paper again. "It says here she needs you to go check on the shop this year, or else."

I snatch the letter away from her just in time to avoid her flour dust tainting the paper. "Or else what? Look, Grams was amazing, but her memory wasn't entirely reliable at the end. She probably didn't remember she had already sold the store when she wrote these letters or something."

"Maybe," she says, but it doesn't sound like she believes it. "I don't know. If my grandmother was sending me nutcrackers *after she died*, and she insisted I check in on her old bookstore, I'd fucking do it." She warily eyes the box holding the teething Father Christmas. "Especially if the request came with a thing looking like *that*. That's a threat, if ever I saw one."

It's not. It can't be. Grams could not have had this level of foresight. She was my grandmother, not an oracle for crying out loud. And yet, I have a weird, tingly feeling about this in the back of my brain. Something doesn't seem right.

I shrug it off. "There's no way it's even still standing," I repeat, though with less conviction this time.

Natalia raises her eyebrows pointedly. "How would you know? You've avoided your hometown like the plague for the past decade."

Longer, but I'm not about to split hairs.

"What's the harm?" she continues. "Just go, check it out, and appease Grams. You want to keep her happy or you might end up with worse than that." She points at the box.

"I don't think there is worse than that."

"Take it back," she warns, her eyes wide as she backs into the kitchen from whence she came. "There's always worse."

I hate to admit that she's probably right, but I'm still not going to Riverbend Springs. Not in a million years.

*You hear that, Grams?* I think. *You can't scare me.*

# Chapter 2

## Lo

Turns out Grams can scare me.

Every single day for two weeks, I get another letter from her in the mail. Each one is increasingly more urgent, bordering on psychosis. This has never happened before. Usually, it's just a nutcracker, a letter about how proud she is of me and how I've done so well for myself, and a gentle reminder that the store is always there for me should I need it...along with a backhanded comment about how it wouldn't kill me to check in every once in a while. Typical Grams.

But these letters are totally unhinged.

*December 5, 20XX*

*My Dearest Gloria,*

*It is time you return home. They say home is where the heart is. That is a crock of shit. Home is Riverbend Springs, and it always will be. You need to go home in order to move forward. Check on The Nook while you're there.*

*Love you forever,*
*Grams*

---

*December 8, 20XX*
*Gloria Dearest,*

*Home for the holidays! Don't you want to go home for the holidays? And I'm not talking about that barebones, whitewashed city apartment you have. That isn't your home. That isn't anyone's home, if we're being honest with ourselves. You might be a big city girl now, but don't forget your roots. Oh, and check in on The Nook for me while you're there.*
*Love you forever,*
*Grams*

She never did quite understand that Aurora isn't the big city. Though, to her, I suppose it might seem like it. But if I were to refer to it that way to anyone living here, I'd get laughed out of town. With Chicago only an hour away, Aurora is firmly in suburban territory. That never mattered to Grams.

---

*December 14, 20XX*
*Let's dispense with the formalities. I know you have a break coming up. Go home. Go to the bookstore. Your destiny is waiting.*
*Love you forever,*
*Grams*

I do have a break coming up, and when little Johnny's spitball hits me straight in the eye, I know it won't be a moment too soon. The kids are restless. I'm restless. I think the spider that has taken up residence in the corner by the door is also waiting for all of us to clear out so she can have some alone time.

The fact of the matter is, having taught fifth grade for a decade, I'm starting to tire of their antics. Normal teachers would probably think it was endearing that the kids found the spider and named her Charlie and wouldn't let me kill her—ahem, move her outside—for example, but spiders might be the only things that creep me out more than the Father Christmas nutcracker. I have nightmares about walking into my classroom to find that the spider has written words in her web like *fraud, loser,* or my personal favorite, *spinster.* (I did reward my brain for that last one. It was pretty punny, all things considered.)

But every time I try to think of something else I'd rather do, I come up short. The only job I ever had that I really loved was working in The Nook with Grams, but opening a new bookstore would require so much time. And some business sense. And probably a credit core above 500—none of which I have.

And it wouldn't be the same without Grams there. So I won't be doing as she requests, no matter how much I dread going home today to find another posthumous letter from her in my mailbox.

I've avoided calling Mom in on this one because she's always been a bit...eclectic. I'm not sure what she'd say about any of it, but my guess has always been that she'd either believe Grams was, without a doubt, sending me nutcrackers from The Great Beyond, or she'd brush it off as some kind of sign from the universe. It isn't a sign, and I don't think Grams can access her shipping account from the grave, so I've just kind of left Mom out of it.

But when I get home from school, there's no letter from Grams, which is somehow weirder than them showing up every day. It gives me the heebie-jeebies enough that I give in and call Mom for an outsider's perspective.

"Hi, sweetie," she says in her breathy voice. "I was just planning our annual tofu platter for New Year's Day. I was thinking something with red peppers this year? What do you think?"

"That sounds great, Mom." I wince. That does not sound great. In fact, no one in any lifetime has ever said, *"Gosh, I can't wait to get home and have some of Mom's homemade tofu with red peppers,"* but that's not why I'm calling. "I...uh...am actually calling because I want to ask your advice."

"Of course! Just give me one minute..." She draws the words out as she finishes up something on her end. "Okay. You have my undivided attention. What's going on?"

"Well... Ugh," I groan. "This is going to sound really weird."

"You're in luck! I'm really weird. Try me."

I huff a laugh at that. Mom has never minced words, and while she is chaos personified, she has a healthy dose of self-awareness. It's my favorite thing about her.

"Okay." I take a deep breath. "I've been getting letters from Grams."

"Ohh." She draws out the sound. And then I wait. But she doesn't say anything else.

"That's it? Just *ohh*?"

"Well, I don't know what you want me to say, sweetie. You told me you've been getting letters from my dead mother." She pauses. "That might actually be the only thing you could have said that's beyond even my capacity for the bizarre."

I blink a few times trying to collect my thoughts. *Rationality* was not on my list of possible responses from her, so now I'm not quite sure what to do.

Luckily, she keeps talking so I don't have to. "I want to say that I absolutely believe you. You are my child, and I don't think you'd ever lie to me, especially after that one time you snuck back in when you and Liam—"

"*Mom*," I cut her off sharply.

"Of course. We won't talk about that. And I can tell by your voice that you aren't having a mental breakdown, so tell me. What kind of letters are you getting from Grams?"

This is the weird part—the part I'm not sure how she's going to react to. "She's been sending me nutcrackers every year."

There's silence for a moment, and then she explodes. "Shut. The. Front. Door. That is the cutest thing I've ever heard. She still sends you nutcrackers every year even after she died?"

"Mom."

"Ohmygosh I am in love with this. How does she do it? Do you think there's someone somewhere she paid to send these to you?"

"Mom."

"Is there a return address? Maybe you could track whoever it is down and—"

"*Mom,*" I snap again. "The nutcrackers aren't the point. Every year, she sends a letter with them. It's always a nice letter, but it always ends the same way. She asks me to check up on The Nook. And now, she's not only sending me the nutcrackers. There's another letter each day, and each one is getting progressively more and more insistent that I go back to the shop."

"What did today's say?"

"Today is the first day in two weeks I didn't get one."

"Huh. That *is* weird. Does she say why she wants you to go there?"

"No, and I can't possibly think of a reason. She sold it years ago. Surely it's not even still a bookstore anymore. Right?

Mom hums, thinking. "I honestly don't know. I haven't been back there for almost as long as you."

I sigh. "So what do I do?"

"I mean..." She trails off, which she only does when she knows I won't like the answer. "There's really only one thing you can do."

"Cuddle up in my robe with a gingerbread latte and watch a Christmas romance on some streaming network to forget any of this ever happened?"

"Gloria," she scolds. "No. The only thing to do is go back to Riverbend Springs."

"I can't just go back to Riverbend Springs!"

"Why not? I'm going on my annual Christmas trip with my ladies' group, and you have two weeks off coming up. Just go there, check in, see whatever it is she so desperately wants you to see, and be done with the whole thing."

"You're making quite the assumption that I don't have a hot date or some other pressing plans. I'm a very busy woman, you know."

"I want to acknowledge that you believe that's true, sweetie." Her voice teeters the line between soothing and patronizing. "But you know Grams. Once she got a bee in her bonnet about something, she never let it go. So make the drive. Check out the shop. Enjoy some small town Christmas nostalgia. And then maybe she'll leave you alone. It's a win-win."

It's a lose-lose because I don't want to go back. I don't want to see what's left of the shop that meant so much to me in my childhood. I don't want to visit with all the people who never left. And I definitely, most certainly, don't want to risk running into anyone I knew from high school—especially Liam White.

But Mom is right. I don't have a choice. If I want this nonsense to stop, I have to just do what Grams is demanding.

I guess I have to admire the woman's persistence. Even from beyond the grave.

# Chapter 3

## Lo

As soon as I wave goodbye to the last child on the last day of the term, I load all of the Best Teacher Ever mugs, potpourri, and lavender relaxation candles from their parents into my car and swing by my apartment to say a quick goodbye to Natalie and grab my already-packed suitcase. I'm almost out the door when I backtrack and change out of my Friday school spirit wear and into leggings and an oversized sweatshirt that has a picture of a skeleton in a Santa hat. It says, *When you're dead inside, but it's the holiday season.*

I figure Grams would have thought it was funny.

And then I'm on my way. Just under three hours later, I'm crossing over the Mississippi River and into Iowa. Another thirty minutes and I'm passing out the north side of Dubuque, through some farmland, and into Riverbend Springs.

The town is exactly how I remember it. Well not *exactly*. The sign at the border reads:

*Welcome to Riverbend Springs*
*Flowing with Charm Since 1836*
*Population 2,892*

That's two more people than I remembered there being here. Nice to see some growth.

One thing that hasn't changed is how much this town clearly loves Christmas. As I pass through the town square, I'm routed around a giant Christmas tree that stretches well above the tops of the buildings. Liam and I used to joke that the town's Christmas tree was probably proportional to the one in Rockefeller Center if you divided the height of each tree by the population of each town. A pang of nostalgia zings through me, but I swallow that right down. I'm not here to find Liam. I don't particularly want to talk to him ever again. And besides, if he's smart, he's probably long gone from this place by now.

The Riverbend Springs tree is beautiful—a fact I'm forced to admit as I follow the world's slowest boat of a car as it creeps its way around the roundabout where it stands. The tree is lit with those giant, retro bulbs in a rainbow of colors, and there are so many handmade ornaments likely created by the students of the entire school district—kindergarten through senior in high school. It was a tradition every year, complete with a contest for the best ornament from each grade level with the winners announced at the tree lighting. I can't imagine they've changed this in the past fourteen years. A big part of me hopes they haven't.

"Fuck!" I cry out, scrambling to hit my breaks when the car I've been patiently following suddenly stops. I almost lay on my horn until I remember where I am. My horn blasting would likely draw out every single shop owner on Main Street and a good number of their customers so they could see what all the commotion was about.

When my heart descends from my throat, I see what the holdup is. A horse-driven sleigh is clomping through the street. A couple is huddled together in the sleigh under a snow-white blanket, cupping steaming mugs in their mitten-covered hands.

Aww. That's cute.

When they finally pass, the car in front of me starts creeping again. I press my head against the headrest, roll my eyes, and settle in. It takes me another twenty minutes to get to the bed and breakfast on the outskirts of town even though I can see it from the roundabout. At least the scenery is pretty. Each shop has intricately painted windows depicting scenes from *A Christmas Carol,* and the awnings are all adorned with fairy light garlands. Wreaths are hung on the old-timey streetlights, and a light dusting of snow tops everything off.

This town could be on a postcard. Actually, if I stopped in the general store, it probably is.

By the time I get to Maisey's Bed & Breakfast, I've never been so happy to pull into a parking spot in my life. Even so, I take a second to appreciate the huge Victorian mansion with all of its vintage outdoor Christmas decorations in exactly the same places I remember them being in my childhood.

Maisey's has always been a staple tourist destination for people wanting to experience a weekend away. It usually saw a rotation of couples, families, and men on fishing trips from Dubuque. It was also a popular wedding venue, with couples getting hitched in the small chapel in town, then holding cocktail hour in the large first-floor space and usually a reception in the sprawling yard outside when the weather was nice. Somehow, the B&B rarely had any vacancies no matter the time of year, which is unexpected when your town has only one stop sign and everyone has to walk to the post office to get their own mail because there's only one postal worker, and he's swamped.

So when I was looking up places to stay and saw that Maisey had set up a new online booking system and had one room available, I jumped on it. When else would I be able to say that I stayed here? And besides, her bacon-and-egg breakfast casserole was always to die for.

My suitcase bounces on each step as I yank it up to the ornate front door. I can see the white lights of a Christmas tree through the leaded glass panes that line the oak door, and I can smell the traditional balsam scent seeping outward even before I open it and step into the warmth of the foyer.

A little bell jingles over the door as it closes behind me, and a moment later, Maisey's voice comes from somewhere out of sight.

"Just a minute!" she calls.

"No rush," I say, even though I know no one knows the meaning of the word in this town. I pull off my gloves one finger at a time and shove them in the pockets of my black puffer coat before taking in my surroundings. This is another thing that hasn't changed one bit. Every single period-appropriate Christmas decoration is exactly the same as it had always been. It's almost as if I stepped through a time machine when I entered the house. And I absolutely love it.

"Oh my goodness. Gloria Carson, as I live and breathe." Maisey appears in the doorway behind the concierge desk. She looks almost like I remember her too, even though there are a few more wrinkles around her eyes and mouth, and her gray roots are showing more than she ever would have let them before.

I give her a stupid little wave and a nervous laugh. "In the flesh."

"Well, I'll be darned," she breathes, her voice full of awe. "When that reservation came through, I saw your name and I thought to myself, *There's no way that's* our *Gloria Carson.* But Chuck kept saying, 'How many Gloria Carsons do you know?' And I had to admit, I didn't know a single one."

"Aside from my Grams."

I half expect her to say something reflexive about her resting in peace. The other half of me expects to hear about how she's been haunting this place, too. But Maisey doesn't say any of that. She just rushes toward me and pulls my arms away from my sides.

"Let me get a look at you!" she all but squeals. "It's been so long!"

"Not much to look at, I'm afraid." And I'm not—especially when I'm cocooned in a giant puffer coat with my chin-length brown hair peeking out the bottom of one of my mom's hand knit Fair Isle hats. The only thing that might be of any note are my eyes, the same shade of whiskey brown as my Grams and my mom. The true Carson family legacy.

"Nonsense." She waves me off. "You were always a looker, and you still are. Just like your momma."

Heat rises to my cheeks that has nothing to do with the warmth of the fireplace. I never have been very good at taking a compliment.

"Thanks, Maisey," I manage. "So...can I check in?"

She winces. "Um... Well... You can."

"But?" I prompt when she doesn't offer anything further.

"The toilet in that room isn't flushing. The room is fine, but you won't be able to use the bathroom. If you think you won't need it much, you're welcome to use the one in the back of the hardware store until we can get it fixed. But there's no other room available tonight, and we can't get anyone out here until tomorrow at the earliest to look at it and—"

I hold up a hand, palm out to stop the onslaught of information. "You couldn't have called to tell me this?"

"I just discovered it when I was cleaning out the room about an hour ago."

There's no way I'm going into the hardware store in my pajamas every time I need to use the bathroom tonight. And what happens when the store closes? I'm left to my own devices all night long? She gives me a bucket, and I hope for the best? That's less than ideal.

I'm calculating whether or not I have the mental and physical fortitude to drive three hours back home and possibly start getting those letters from Grams again when Maisey makes a strange sound. I look at her, my eyebrows raised in question.

"What?" I ask.

"Well, I was honestly kind of surprised you were staying here at all."

"What do you mean?"

"Your Grams's old place is right up the road," she explains. "Empty. No one has lived in it for years."

My eyebrows practically hurt from how much work they're doing as I frown deeply. "She sold the house when she moved into the nursing home."

"Did she?" Maisey cocks her head in thought.

She knows damn well I'm right. In a town with a population of 2,890—sorry, 2,892—everyone knows everything about everyone. And knowing Maisey, she was probably standing in the street outside Grams's house the day she sold it, dabbing her eyes with a handkerchief and moaning about the end of an era.

"Yes," I say through gritted teeth.

She waves this away as if it's no big deal. "Well, no one has lived there since she left. I can't imagine whoever owns it now will mind if you stay there for one night. You can come back here tomorrow, and everything will be good as new." She scrunches up her face. "Probably. But either way, you shouldn't be driving at night. I think it's going to start snowing again, too. Stay there, and you can make a plan in the morning."

I have so many questions. Namely, who has been paying the bills on that house if no one has lived in it for years? And why?

But I'm suddenly too tired to try to work all this out. And I'm getting the sneaking suspicion that, whatever is going on here with Grams, Maisey is in on it. I wouldn't even be surprised to find out that the toilet in the room works just fine and this is some ploy to get me to check on Grams's house, too.

"Fine," I say, resigned. "I don't suppose you have a spare key?"

Maisey's delight at my agreement fades quickly. "I don't. Shoot." She thinks for a moment, then snaps her fingers. "Stay here. I'll be right back."

She's out the door without even taking her coat with her before I can ask where she's going. More confused than ever, I drag my suitcase to an oversized armchair next to the roaring fireplace and have a seat. But before too long, Maisey is back, her round cheeks pink from the cold.

"Here you go!" She holds out a key.

Giving her a quizzical look, I take it from her. "Where did you get this?"

"From John! At the hardware store," she explains.

"I know who John is. Why did he have a key to Grams's old place?"

"He has keys to everyone's place," she says as if this isn't a massive invasion of privacy. "He's also the locksmith."

I shouldn't push it when she doesn't seem to see anything wrong with it, but this is massively unsafe. "That absolutely does not mean he should have keys to everyone's home."

Maisey rolls her eyes. "Ten years ago, he asked that everyone give him their keys to copy so it'd be easier for him to run the hardware store and help people get into their houses when they had been locked out. It happens a lot, you know. Anyway, he doesn't just have a weird collection of people's keys. Everyone voluntarily handed them over."

"That's not better," I mumble, but I also know better than to argue with Riverbend Springs logic. And besides, not even the prospect of staying in Grams's empty house that John somehow has a spare key to is as creepy as that Father Christmas nutcracker. That thing still haunts my dreams.

It doesn't really matter anyway. With any luck, I won't even need the room at Maisey's tomorrow night. I'll wake up early, check in on The Nook, and be back in Illinois by noon.

"Right. Anyway. Thanks Maisey." I stand and put my gloves back on before dragging my suitcase to the door.

"Good luck, Gloria!" She waves enthusiastically. "See you tomorrow!"

I flash her a tight smile before rolling the suitcase out onto the porch and thumping it back down the stairs to my car.

Grams's old house is only a few minutes away, but I have to work hard to shove down all of the memories that start popping up on the drive. The creek I used to sit next to every summer, relaxing and soaking in sunshine, passes on my right. On my left, the house I lived in with mom, now with a new family sitting down to dinner in the dining room window. At the end of the driveway is still the giant boulder Mom always meant to have removed—the one that Liam backed his car into once in a hurry to get home before curfew. I wonder if the scuff of blue paint is still there. I bet it is.

I groan, rubbing at my chest with one hand while my other steadies the steering wheel. I didn't expect coming back to Riverbend Springs to hurt so much.

No matter. By this time tomorrow, I'll be gone, and hopefully Grams will leave me alone so I'll never have to think about this town again.

I pull into the driveway of the single-story ranch style house a few moments later. When I get inside, I flick on a light. Miraculously, it works. I can't decide if I'm surprised or not that Grams's house looks almost exactly the way I remember it. It smells like it used to, too. Even the furniture appears untouched. And everything is immaculately clean, as if there has been a cleaning service in and out of here very week.

A picture of Grams, Mom, and me hangs on the wall next to the door. In it, I'm about eleven years old. I remember that time. No one could persuade me to smile for a camera. A thousand dollars couldn't get me to crack a grin. But Mom had it in her head that we needed family pictures, and for weeks beforehand, she'd use various tactics to get me to promise I'd try to look happy. Nothing worked—not begging, not bribing, not even her crocodile tears.

Grams had been conspicuously quiet throughout the whole ordeal. But the day of our little photo shoot, when the photographer was pointing her camera in our direction, I had my arms folded tight across my chest. I was feeling particularly awkward about puberty in general that day. None of my favorite outfits felt right or looked good when I put them on, so there was no way I was going to smile. I was not in a smiling mood.

Before the shutter on the camera closed, Grams tipped her chin to a grove of trees off in the distance and said, "I don't trust those trees. They seem shady."

The result was Mom squinting and puffing out her cheeks, unable to hold back her laughter, and me smiling—albeit close-lipped—but a smile nonetheless. Grams is the only one in the picture who looks normal. We decided to keep it anyway for posterity. Plus, it was probably the only photo from that year in which I didn't look like I'd give anything to be anywhere else.

Funny, because now I'd give a lot to be back there again.

I run a finger over the top of the picture frame and peer at it closely. Not a speck of dust. Grams wasn't even that exacting in her cleaning. Definitely a cleaning service, then. But why?

"Okay, Grams," I say to the empty space. "You got me here. What the hell do you want?"

The only answer I get is the sound of the central heating kicking on and the wind picking up outside.

"Well, the heat works." I sigh as I roll my suitcase down the hall. I stop in one of the bathrooms to flush the toilet. "And the toilet flushes." It's an improvement from Maisey's at least.

I continue on into the guest room. Staying in Grams's old room would be a step too far, I decide. I change into a sweatshirt and sweatpants, then dig around in my suitcase for my cozy socks and the bottle of wine I packed. It's a screw top, so I open it up and find a glass in the cabinet next to the sink and pour myself a hefty serving before bringing it back to the bedroom to snuggle under the comforter with a book. I read until my eyelids are too heavy to keep them open any longer.

Around 3:00 in the morning, I wake up shivering. The wind is howling outside, and no matter what I do to the thermostat, nothing happens.

The heat is out. Of course it is.

Suddenly, a not-functioning toilet doesn't seem so bad. But it's too late at night to wake Maisey up, so I grab as many blankets as I can find and set myself up next to the electric fireplace to stay warm until I can get the fuck out of here in the morning.

# Chapter 4

## Liam

FROM THE BOOTH IN the back of Jesse's Diner, I check my watch and pull my faded blue baseball hat lower over my face. Tracy is late. She's always late. Five years of dealing with her and I don't know why I continually show up on time when I know she's going to be thirty minutes behind schedule without a text or a call letting me know. It happens every time, without fail.

I must be grumbling when Jesse comes over to refill my coffee, because he chuckles as he pours. "It's not like this is out of the ordinary for her."

"I know," I say gruffly, cupping the mug with my hands.

"Can I get you anything while you wait?"

I only shake my head, and Jesse shrugs. He turns to walk away but thinks better of it and slides into the seat across from me. It takes a lot of effort not to roll my eyes as his ass slips across the pleather seat cushion, making a squeaking noise as he settles in.

"Sure, Jesse. Have a seat."

"Thanks, I will," he returns tartly. "I heard some interesting news from Maisey this morning."

"I don't care." I bring the scalding, burnt coffee to my lips and take a sip. It's no use, though. Jesse is going to tell me the news whether I want to hear it or not. He and I have been friends since we were on the baseball team together in high school, so I know when he gets that shit-eating grin on his face, there's no stopping him from ruining my day.

He laughs again as he turns a mug upright and pours himself a cup of coffee. "I think you will."

I arch an eyebrow at him. "Don't you have work to do?"

"I own the place. I have employees for that."

"The fact that you're someone's actual employer is all the proof I need that I'm on the wrong timeline," I say into my coffee. The truth is that Jesse saved this place from going under when he bought it last year. It would have been devastating for Riverbend Springs to lose the diner. So many other businesses from our childhood have folded—the community theater, the photography studio, the flower shop. But thanks to the thirty-somethings who stayed or came back to make Riverbend Springs their home, the downtown is seeing a revitalization of sorts. We're buying businesses and doing what we can to keep the community alive. Even I can admit that's pretty cool.

"Shut up." He rolls his eyes. "You own a whole-ass construction company. You have to be, like, an adult to do that. Which you are not."

"I'm older than you."

"By two months. Now do you want to hear this news or not?"

"I already told you. No." I take a big gulp of coffee hoping it will make him less annoying. It doesn't work.

He leans forward and lowers his voice conspiratorially. "I'm going to tell you, but I need you to swallow that coffee first so you don't spit it in my face."

I stare at him, unblinking, as I hold the hot coffee in my mouth for as long as I can stand it. Reluctantly I swallow, and it warms my esophagus all the way down.

"Maisey told me Lo Carson is in town."

It takes a lot not to react to his words. I haven't heard that name in over a decade. Not since I ruined our friendship by wanting more. She and I fought, and she left for college two months early and didn't return any of my texts or phone calls for over a year before I gave up.

Jesse regards me for a moment, then one side of his mouth turns up as his eyebrows lower in a skeptical look. "You have no reaction to this?"

"Why should I react?"

"You two were attached at the hip from the time you were born until the time she disappeared."

"She didn't disappear," I protest. "She went to school."

"Right. Fine. Whatever you want to tell yourself. And you know what? You would have been prepared for this if you showed your face more than once every week to meet Tracy here. People have been speculating about this for a while now."

"What does *speculating* mean?" A little voice comes from my right.

Jesse and I both startle as we turn toward the little girl standing next to the booth. Her brown pigtails are topped with sparkly red and green bows, and she's wearing the ugliest Christmas sweater I've ever seen. It's lime green with an appliqué of a shirtless Santa in sunglasses and a reindeer swimsuit. On the top, it says, *Seas-ons Greetings!*

"It means *guessing*. Did your mom buy you that sweater?" I ask.

She scowls. "Yes. And I'm *speculating* you don't like it."

"Hmm," I hum. "Smart kid."

Rolling her eyes, she scoots into the booth next to me. "Dad." She draws the word out with exasperation.

Jesse laughs. "Woah, Mia. When did you turn fifteen?"

Mia shifts so she's sitting on her knees and glares at him. "I'm not fifteen, Jesse. I'm five."

"Could have fooled me."

"Me too." Tracy comes up to the table, shimmying as if she can shake the cold off of her. "A lot more snow on the ground today than there was yesterday."

"All the better to play in, right Noodle?" I wink at Mia, who giggles and bounces up and down excitedly.

"Can we go sledding?"

"I was hoping we could camp out all day outside the diner and make snow-balls to ambush Jesse with after he closes."

Mia scrunches up her face in thought. "Nah. I'd rather go sledding."

"Good looking out for me, kiddo." Jesse slides out of the booth and picks up the carafe of coffee. He raises it to Tracy in question, who shakes her head. "I'll leave y'all to it. Wouldn't want to be accused of slacking on the job."

"Never," I grumble as Tracy slides into the spot Jesse had just been occupying. He saunters away toward the counter so he can chat with some other unsuspecting customer.

"Mom," Mia says, still bouncing on her knees. "Can I eat at the counter? And can I order chocolate chip pancakes?"

Tracy shakes her head. "You ate a donut at home, remember? Eggs and fruit."

Mia makes a whining noise so high-pitched, I have to rub my ear when it stops. "But I'm on *vacation.*"

"You're on a break from school. It's not a vacation. Eggs and fruit, but you can eat it at the counter while I talk to your dad."

"Fine." She hops out of the booth and stomps away, resigned.

Tracy's blue eyes follow her until she climbs up on one of the red-upholstered stools at the counter and waits for Jesse to take her order.

"He's going to give her the pancakes," she says. "I don't know why I try."

"He'll probably give her eggs and fruit, too."

"She won't eat them." Tracy shrugs and turns back to me. "Oh well. She's your problem for the next week."

I idly stir my coffee as I eye her across the table. "I promise she won't come back to you entirely loaded with sugar." Smirking, I add, "Just a little loaded."

Tracy shoots me an annoyed look, but then her face breaks into a wide smile. She really is a beautiful woman, and Mia takes after her in so many ways. Sleek brown hair, big blue eyes, cheekbones that could cut glass. The only thing Mia gets from me are my dimples and a desire to work with my hands. That kid is always tinkering with something. It drives Tracy nuts, but I love helping her take things apart and put them back together again.

Tracy and I knew each other in high school, but we didn't really get to know each other until…well…about five years ago. We started talking at a bar, one thing led to another, the condom broke, and five years later we're here, sharing custody of our daughter in the most amicable way possible. We tried to make it work when we found out she was pregnant, but Tracy has a winning personality. She's outgoing and loves being social. I, on the other hand, would be happy to live in a cave and never come out. I wasn't good for her—even I could see that. So we decided to raise her separately, but together. That's how we defined it, anyway. I was still at every doctor's appointment. I was there for her birth and every special occasion after that. But she switches houses every week, and we trade holidays. This year, I get Mia for Christmas, and even my cold, black heart is excited for it.

"You sure you want her for the whole first week of winter break?" Tracy cocks an eyebrow as if she can't believe it.

"Yeah," I say simply. The truth is, I have a whole itinerary planned. I'm excited for uninterrupted time with my kid, even though I don't say any more than that.

"A man of few words, as usual." She sighs. "And you have off this whole week, too?"

I nod. "Not a lot of construction happening with it being so cold. Just some odd jobs around town. Maisey's got a toilet problem. Jesse wanted me to refinish some tables. Stuff like that."

"Good," she says. "Good, good."

I can tell she's gearing up to say something else by the way her lips twist to the side and her eyes narrow. If I were a betting man, I'd put money on what she's going to say next.

"I heard Lo Carson is back in town."

Yep. Should have put money on it.

I grunt something incomprehensible into my coffee. Tracy rolls her eyes. And that's when I glance toward the counter to check on Mia—who is, indeed, shoveling chocolate chip pancakes into her mouth. Only, she's talking to a woman I don't immediately recognize. That is, not until Mia points toward our table. The woman looks over, and I'm met with the brown hair, heart-shaped face, and whiskey brown eyes of Lo Carson.

Out of the corner of my eye, I see Tracy turn to look, then spin back around to face me. She laughs darkly. "Oh, this is going to be fun."

# Chapter 5

## Lo

IF I HAD BEEN able to think beyond finding coffee and food after freezing my ass off for four hours, I would have known better than to go inside the diner. It was always a gathering place for everyone on weekend mornings, and clearly today is no different. Mercifully, there's a spot open at the counter, but almost as soon as I slide onto the stool, a little girl with pigtails and a neon sweater pops up next to me, shifting so she can sit taller on her knees.

"Jesse, can I have chocolate chip pancakes?" She flashes a brilliant smile complete with adorable dimples, and for a moment it's like I'm looking at a younger, female version of Liam. I shake my head quickly because that can't be right. I'm just delirious from the cold and lack of sustenance.

"What did your mom say?" Jesse calls from the other side of the counter. His messy blond hair has been tamed slightly over the years, but he's still got the same boyish charm he always had. He glances at me, then does a double take and smirks but doesn't say anything more.

I knew Jesse decently well in high school. He and Liam were friends, so we all hung out quite a bit. From the look on his face, he knew I was in town. That checks out. The prodigal daughter returning would be the type of news that would take less than twenty-four hours to spread here.

The little girl sighs and slumps dramatically over the counter. "She said I had to eat eggs and fruit."

Jesse makes his way over to this side of the counter. He dips his chin at me. "Hey, Lo," he says quietly. "Good to see you."

Without another word, he turns over a mug and pours me a cup of burnt-smelling coffee. I've never been so grateful in my life. For the coffee, sure, but also for the fact that it doesn't seem like he's going to make a big deal about the fact that I'm here.

He wipes at a spot on the counter and winks at the kid. "What about eggs, fruit, *and* chocolate chip pancakes?"

The kid pops up, her face brightening. "Oh! That could work."

"Coming right up." Jesse turns to the window to the kitchen behind him and calls out the order, then he faces me. "Anything for you, Lo?"

I chew on the inside of my cheek, thinking. "Do you still do those holly jolly waffles that Bea used to have every year?"

He flashes me a wide smile. "Of course I do. Can't mess with tradition."

"I'll have that, then."

Jesse calls out my order, then moves away to take care of some of the other customers. I can't help but notice how he thrives in this role. He's so outgoing and personable, and he's always had a smile that makes everyone feel welcome. I wouldn't have guessed he'd be happy staying in this town, but it seems like he is.

"My mom says those holly jolly waffles will give you a heart attack," the little girl next to me says.

"Your mom sounds like a killjoy," I mutter into my coffee, hoping that's the last I have to hear from her.

With remarkable speed, Jesse deposits plates of food in front of both of us. They must have premade food in the kitchen ready to go, but I don't care how fresh it is. The waffles look amazing. They're piled high with whipped cream and dusted with powdered sugar to look like snow. Raspberry sauce drizzles out the sides, and green sprinkles adorn all of it.

"My name's Mia." She interrupts the bite I had halfway to my mouth by sticking a little hand straight in my face as if she wants to shake. I notice a few specks of glitter caught on her sweaty palm, but I take it to shake anyway.

"I'm Lo."

"Lo?" She tilts her head and regards me with huge blue eyes. "That's a funny name." Doesn't seem to bother her too much though, as she pushes her eggs to the side and takes a giant, chocolatey bite of pancake.

"It's short for Gloria," I say impatiently. "Where are your parents?"

That's when she indicates a booth in the back where a man and woman sit. I recognize the woman—Tracy McCollough. And she's exactly as gorgeous as she was in high school when she was voted best dancer, most school spirited, and most likely to break hearts.

That last one wasn't real, but it probably could have been.

But I can't be too preoccupied with her because across the booth is none other than Liam White. His shoulders are hunched over a cup of coffee that's cradled in his hands. He's wearing a faded blue baseball cap pulled low on his forehead, but the black hair curling out from under it and the brown eyes locked on me are unmistakable.

And then it hits me like a ton of bricks. My heart practically stops, and my stomach bottoms out. "Hold on," I say to the little girl. "Tracy McCollough is your mom? And Liam White is your *dad*?" I cringe inwardly as soon as I say it because what if it's Tracy White now? Am I about to find out my former best friend not only has a kid but is married, too?

I guess he got over me eventually. Which is good. Great. Wonderful, even.

Mia bounces on the stool, which gives me next to zero information. "Yeah! Do you know them?"

I don't get a chance to respond because Tracy is already out of her seat and stalking toward us, clearly struggling to hide a grin.

This is not going to be fun.

"Lo Carson. You sure are a sight for sore eyes." Tracy stands behind Mia, steadies her, and pulls the plate of eggs back in front of the kid all in one fluid movement. It's the practiced move of someone entrenched in motherhood—the kind she probably didn't even have to think about—and I try to ignore the twinge of sadness that comes over me. I missed a lot, apparently. And yeah, that's on me, but it still makes me more than a little upset.

"It's more likely I'm making your eyes sore," I return. It wasn't even a good joke, but Tracy is so nice that she laughs anyway.

"Maisey's not treating the guests well?"

"What?" I frown before I remember that this is a small town, and everyone has probably known for weeks that I was coming back and exactly where I was planning to stay. "Oh, no. I'm sure her accommodations are as wonderful as always. Apparently the toilet wasn't working in my room, so I stayed at Grams's old place. But the heat went out in the middle of the night, so..."

Mia must decide that the grown-up conversation is too boring for her because she side-eyes her mom, takes a tiny bite of eggs and a piece of fruit, and then dives back into her pancakes.

"Liam mentioned something about fixing a toilet over there," Tracy muses. At least Maisey was telling the truth, then.

Just when I'm about to excuse myself from the conversation and bury myself in my sugar-covered waffles, Tracy cocks an eyebrow at me. "You need someone to fix your heater."

It's a statement, not a question, but I answer anyway. "Oh, no. I'm just here to—" How do I explain that my dead grandmother has been sending me messages from beyond the grave urging me to check in on this place? This isn't my mom we're talking about. No one here would believe me. Especially if how they felt about us when I was in high school is any indication.

My gaze flicks to Liam, who isn't looking at us anymore. Good. That's for the best.

I settle on telling her, "I'll be gone by tonight. I'm only here for the day."

"Nonsense," she says, then calls over her shoulder. "Liam, come over here."

Liam hesitates, but he must realize resistance is futile because he drags himself out of the booth with what looks like great effort. When he stands to his full height, it occurs to me that I must have forgotten how tall he is. Even in high school, he was a head taller than almost all the other guys. When we were both standing and he'd bring me into a hug, I used to be able to press my face into his chest and breathe in the warm, spiced scent of his cologne.

I wonder if he still smells like that.

He's dressed in a well-worn, lined flannel jacket with a basic white T-shirt underneath. His jeans are dark-wash denim slung low over his hips, but have clearly faded with wear, especially around the pockets where he now jams his hands inside. He takes his time shuffling over to us and when he finally gets here, he stares at a fixed spot on the ground.

It's the same posture he took before he told me he was in love with me. Before I freaked out and blew it up in his face, too afraid to take that leap before we both left for school.

That memory comes crashing into me out of nowhere. And here, I thought I had locked it up and thrown away the key.

"Liam, look who's here," Tracy says, a fake smile plastered on her face.

"I have eyes," he grumbles.

She elbows him, hard. He grunts and scuffs the toe of his shoe against the ground.

"Hi, Lo. Nice to see you again," he mutters, barely audible and definitely insincere.

It's cool. I didn't want to see him either, so I get it. "Hey, Liam. Same. I was just going to eat these and run, so—"

"Lo needs the heater fixed at her Grams's old house." Tracy bounces forward on her toes, almost giddy. Kind of a weird move for the mother of his child—and maybe his wife—to be making, but it's still not the weirdest thing I've experienced in the past twenty-four hours, so I choose to ignore it.

"I really don't," I protest, but Liam cuts me off.

"When did the heat go out?" He finally looks at me, frowning. His gaze is so full of concern that it catches me completely off guard. He looks me up and down as if he's searching for any sign of frostbite or other injury.

I shiver, but not because of the cold. Sure feels like the heat is on right now.

"Uh," I hedge, scrambling for a crumb of intelligent thought. "Around three in the morning."

He studies me again with the same intensity, then nods. "I'll be over in an hour."

"Oh, no. I—"

"It's no trouble." He's back to looking anywhere but at me. He turns his attention to his daughter. "Ready to go, Noodle?"

Dammit, he even has an adorable nickname for her. Of course he does. He's her father—a fact I still can't wrap my head around.

Mia takes one last giant bite of pancake, then jumps off the stool and waves at me on her way out the door. Liam, on the other hand, doesn't even look at me.

I start recalculating my schedule in my head. Liam will be there in an hour. Probably another hour before it's fixed. I can still get to The Nook by noon and be on the road by two. No problem.

Jesse saunters over again, shaking his head with dismay. "Don't feel bad, Lo. He treats everyone that way."

Tracy sits on the stool Mia had just occupied and starts to eat her daughter's almost untouched eggs and fruit. I look her up and down, and...yep. She's still really fucking pretty.

I tip my head in her direction. "I kind of doubt he treats her that way."

Tracy snorts, but it's such a cute, delicate sound that it doesn't do anything to take away from her attractiveness. "You'd be surprised." She shakes her head as if coming out of a trance, then shovels a few more bites into her mouth. "Anyway, have a great day, Lo. I have to get to work. But I'll see you around, okay?" She wiggles her fingers in a goodbye as she stands and shifts her purse on her shoulder.

"You won't," I call after her on her way out the door. "I'm leaving tonight." If I say it enough times, maybe it'll be true.

"Bye!" she calls as if she didn't hear me or didn't care.

Jesse watches her walk out, and then he pours me another cup of coffee. "Better eat up. You're going to want to be back by the time Liam gets to your Grams's house."

"Do I?" I ask.

I'm not quite sure if it's a rhetorical question or not, but Jesse just shakes his head and laughs as he walks away.

# Chapter 6

## Lo

I GET BACK TO Grams's house with about ten minutes to spare, completely hopped up on sugar and caffeine. Telling myself that's why my heart is racing and it has nothing to do with seeing Liam again, I try to make myself as presentable as I can while my hands are almost turning blue from the cold and I'm still wearing three layers under a puffer coat. I'm not cleaning myself up for Liam, though. I haven't cared about Liam in a long time.

That's not true. Even I can't be delusional enough to believe that. I cared about him deeply. So much that, when he pushed for more, I was so scared. Long-distance relationships never work. Everyone knows that. And we were headed off to separate colleges. His timing was so bad. I got angry because I was afraid, he got angry because he was embarrassed. And then I felt I had no choice but to leave and never look back. At least, that's what I thought at the time.

But I can't think about that now. Not when Liam is on his way.

The doorbell rings. Scratch that. Liam is here.

Checking myself one more time in the mirror, I rush to answer the door. Before I can say hello, Mia bursts through and into the front room. She stops short, hands on her hips, and looks around with a hyper-critical eye.

"I smell glitter." She sniffs the air. "Where is it?"

"Um...what?" I look at Liam helplessly.

He shakes his head as he stomps his snow-covered boots on the mat at the front entrance. "Mia, shoes off."

She huffs in annoyance, then sits down and pulls off her shoes before marching off on an apparent quest for glitter.

"I had to bring her," he says to me. "She's with me this week."

"She's with..." I trail off before I realize what he's saying. "Oh. You and Tracy aren't—"

"No," he cuts me off. He looks around me to peer into the living room. Apparently satisfied, he lowers his voice. "She got pregnant, but... We never... We tried to make it work. It just didn't..."

Liam was always a man of few words. I liked that about him—I never felt the need to force conversation. Being with him was a comfort, maybe especially when we weren't saying anything. But there were times like this when he couldn't find the words to say what he wanted. It was adorable then, and I hate to admit that it's adorable now.

I glance behind me to make sure she's not listening. "She wasn't planned?"

"No." Liam's eyes go wide and he shakes his head. "I don't think I'd have seen Tracy after that night if she hadn't..." He shrugs, his features softening. "But Mia is the best thing that ever happened to me, you know?"

I nod slowly. I certainly don't know anything about having a child, but I work with them all day long, and I can see how they could change someone's life for the better even if they haven't changed mine. "She seems like a great kid." I smile in a way that I hope is reassuring. It must be, because Liam's shoulders relax and he half-smiles back.

We stand there for a moment, until a large crash comes from the living room, followed by a joyous cackle.

"Jackpot!" Mia cries. "So. Much. Glitter."

"I guess that answers my question about whether or not Grams's craft closet is intact," I mutter. Liam laughs softly, and I sigh, looking around at the foyer. "You don't know who has kept this place in mint condition, do you?"

He frowns, following my gaze and landing on the picture of us laughing. A small smile tugs at his lips as he huffs. "It's exactly the same."

"Yeah." I narrow my eyes at him because he didn't answer the question. "It's weird."

His gaze lands on me and he cocks an eyebrow. "Christmas magic?"

"I'm skeptical."

"Does that mean you're guessing?" Mia has suddenly appeared at my side, clutching a bottle of sparkling glitter in each hand. I jump in surprise, but she just grins wider.

"That's *speculate*," Liam corrects. "*Skeptical* means she's not sure."

"Oh." Mia frowns at me. "Skeptical about what?"

"About Christmas magic," I tell her. Probably best not to get into all my suspicions about Grams's afterlife activities with a precocious five-year-old. With glitter.

"Well, no wonder," she spits out. "This place isn't Christmasy at all. You need help, and fast. Good thing I'm here!" She raises the glitter above her head and shakes the bottles. I send up a prayer of gratitude that they're still capped.

"Nope." Liam gently guides her toward the closet. "We're here to fix the heater, and then we are leaving. And you need to pick up the mess you managed to make after being here for only ten minutes."

"Dad," she whines. "You can't not have any decorations on Christmas. It's in three days! There's not much time!"

Liam presses his lips into a thin line and points at the craft supplies strewn across the floor. "Pick them up, please."

"If it makes you feel any better, I won't be here for Christmas," I assure her. "I'm just here to take care of some business, and then I'll be on my way."

"Oh." She actually looks disappointed as she surveys the craft supplies. "Well...can I keep some of these anyway?"

"Knock your socks off, kid."

Liam shoots me a look, but I just shrug. I won't be needing any of them. Better they don't go to waste.

While he goes down to the basement to do whatever it is he needs to do, I bend down to help Mia gather up the supplies she wants. She selects a still-wrapped pack of construction paper, some stick-on sequins, and of course every tube of glitter she can find. We pack it away in a box for her, and I shove the rest of it back in the closet as a whooshing sound comes from the vents. Liam clomps up the stairs and closes the basement door behind him.

"That was fast," I remark.

"It was just the breaker."

"Oh," I say as if I have any idea what that means. "So you're done?" It makes me inexplicably sad that they'll be leaving so soon after they got here. It shouldn't. When I got into town last night, I didn't want to see Liam at all, and I didn't even know Mia existed. But now that they're here, I don't really want them to go.

"Yep," he says simply. And I guess it is that simple. He came to do a job, and the job is done.

"Can I pay you or something?" I ask. That's what you do for people who do jobs, right?

Liam scoffs at me. "Don't be ridiculous. I don't charge friends to reset a breaker."

As if he just realized what he called me, his brown eyes grow a fraction wider and settle on me. We stare at each other like that for a moment before he cocks an eyebrow in question.

I had thought what he did was unforgivable. I had also thought I'd never see him again, and while I wasn't fine with that, I had come to terms with it. But now that he's here, looking at me with an expression so much like the ones he used to make when we were kids, I can't find it in me to be as angry as I was. Maybe it's true that time heals all wounds.

"Right." I nod once. "Thanks."

"What business do you have here?" Mia asks. "My mom says no one has business here, and that's why she works in Dubuque."

I laugh a little too loudly, glad the tension is broken. "Well, I'm here to check on my Grams's bookstore. If it even is still a bookstore. She...um...wanted me to."

Mia's blue eyes light up with excitement. "I love bookstores! We go to one downtown all the time because Daddy—"

"Okay, Noodle," Liam cuts her off. "Let's not take up more of Miss Lo's time."

Cringing, I stand. "Don't call me that. My students try to call me that sometimes, and I have to remind them I don't teach preschool."

Liam's face cracks into a huge grin. "You're a teacher."

I can't help but smile back. His smile has always been contagious, on the rare occasion anyone gets to see a whole one. I see that hasn't changed, either.

"Yeah."

"That's great. That's what you always wanted."

I don't have the heart to tell him it's not all it's cracked up to be, so I just nod. "Yep."

He looks at me strangely for another second, then bends down to pick up an armful of craft supplies. "Well, we'll get out of your hair so you can do what you need to do and get back to your family for Christmas," he says.

"Oh," I giggle nervously as I follow them to the door. "No. My mom's on a trip, and my roommate is back in Kentucky with her family. It'll just be me this year." It's just me every year, but somehow that feels too sad to admit.

Mia gasps. "What? Noooo," she wails. "You can't be alone on Christmas."

"Oh." I pat her on the shoulder. She's so sweet. "It's okay. I don't mind."

She looks up at Liam, and for a second, I think she might be about to cry. "Dad, can we—"

"Noodle, Lo is a grown woman. She can do what she wants for the holiday."

Turning to me, she bunches her brows into the most adorable frown. "Do you want to be alone on Christmas?"

I kneel down so I'm eye-level with her. "It's not so bad," I say, then I lean in to whisper, "I get to eat all the pie myself." I wink at her, and she smiles, but it doesn't quite reach her eyes.

"Come on." Liam holds out her shoes. "We have a toilet to look at."

She sits down right there in the foyer to pull her shoes on. "And *then* can we go sledding?"

"Yes, then we can go sledding."

Shoes in place, she pops up and cheers before running down the steps toward Liam's truck.

Liam lingers for another minute, drinking me in as if he might never see me again. "See you around, Lo," he says finally.

"Yeah. See you," I return. Except I might not. And I don't know why that makes me sadder than the prospect of being alone on Christmas this year.

# Chapter 7

## Liam

I'm in another world when we leave Lo. It was completely disconcerting being in that house again, and not a tchotchke out of place. Everything was exactly as I remember it from our childhood, down to the pictures on the walls and the doilies on the arms of the couch. Cleaner, though. Which is somehow even more strange.

Though, knowing Lo's Grams, she had a plan for that house just like she had a plan for everything else.

Lo keeps saying she's leaving tonight, and I'm in my own head about it. Now that I've seen her again, I don't want to let her go. She disappeared so suddenly all those years ago and never gave me a chance to apologize for what I had done. I was in love with her then, and I thought it was the perfect time to see if we could make a relationship work. She was scared of long distance, and she knew her mom would be leaving town as soon as she did. It was unclear if or when she'd be coming back aside from a weekend or holiday here or there. Convinced a long-distance relationship would ruin our friendship, she turned me down.

The irony of it was that our friendship was ruined anyway. We fought about it, yelled at each other. We both said some things we didn't mean, and she left for college early.

Grams assured me Lo was fine and she'd be back eventually. Grams's steadfastness was only a little reassuring, so when I went away to school, I tried to put Lo out of my mind. *Tried* being the operative word. It didn't work. And it especially didn't work when I came back here and all those memories came flooding back...

I definitely can't put her out of my mind now. She's as gorgeous as she ever was. Maybe more. Those whiskey brown eyes I could get lost in, that tiny nose I used to run my finger down when she was being especially cute, those pink, pouty lips. I always wondered what those lips tasted like, but before I confessed my love to her, I was too nervous to ever find out. Turns out that was for the best. If I had kissed her and she had left like that, it would have shattered my heart. As it was, she broke it in two. But at least without having kissed her, I was able to put it back together. Mostly.

I don't want to say Tracy was my consolation prize. That wouldn't be fair to her. But when I came back from college to start my company in Dubuque, I was lonely. So I slept with her. We both wanted it...a lot. She was great. She *is* great. She's just not Lo. But it was abundantly clear Lo wasn't coming back, no matter how much I believed in Grams's continued encouragement. And now, here we are.

*"Trust the process,"* Grams would say. *"She just needs to decide this is where she wants to be."*

Now Lo is here, and she still doesn't seem like she wants to stay.

"Dad?" Mia asks tentatively from the back seat, breaking me out of my reverie.

"Yeah, Noodle?"

"Lo seemed nice."

"She is." I drum my fingers against the steering wheel.

"And pretty."

*She is,* I think. "What are you getting at, kid?"

Mia sighs heavily. She's such a drama queen, a fact that has endeared her to almost every person in Riverbend Springs, but I know better. She's angling toward something, and I just have to wait it out until she tells me.

I check the rearview mirror to find her looking in it to meet my gaze. Now that she has my attention, she flops dramatically over the arm of her booster and whines, "It's not right that she's going to be alone for Christmas."

Laughing at her antics, I shake my head. "Why do you care so much? You don't even know her."

"Yeah, but you do. You said she's your friend."

Damn, this kid misses nothing. "I did say that."

"Friends don't let friends be alone on Christmas."

I rub my lips together and narrow my eyes. "What do you want me to do?" There's about a fifty-fifty chance Mia has a half-decent plan cooked up already. I'll take those odds.

She raises her eyebrows with a devious smirk. "The Christmas Market is tonight. You should invite her."

I wait a minute in silence thinking there's more to this plan. Clearly there isn't.

"There are three days until Christmas," I remind her as I pull into a parking spot near Maisey's. "That's just tonight. What else you got?"

Rolling her eyes in her typical, dramatic fashion, she groans. "I don't know *yet.*" She draws out the word as if it's painful to have to explain this to me. "We're just buying some time. And besides, who can resist the Christmas Market? It's magical!" She throws her arms wide on the last word, a wistful look on her face.

Lo and I used to love walking around the Christmas Market. We'd split up and buy each other something small, then meet to get hot chocolate and exchange our little gifts. It *was* magical, but I don't think the magic had a lot to do with Christmas.

I think it had to do with her.

Unbuckling my seatbelt and hopping down from the truck, I sigh. When I open the door to help Mia down, she bounces her eyebrows at me.

"You got a better plan?" she asks.

"It should disturb me how invested you are in this." I heft her up from her armpits and set her on the ground.

"You don't," she sings.

She's right. I don't. But I also don't want Lo to be trapped here with us if she doesn't want to be. That would be worse.

So all I can tell my kid as I shut her door is, "I'll think about it."

# Chapter 8

## Lo

I'M NOT EXACTLY DRAGGING my feet on my way to The Nook, but now that the time has come to go there, I'm almost afraid to do it. What if it really is a parking lot? Or a law office? Or worse, what if it's one of those touristy shops that sell those garish, air-brushed T-shirts?

I don't know why Riverbend Springs would have one of those shops, but it would be terrible if The Nook was one now.

The Nook and Granny is—was?—situated on Jefferson Avenue, one of the side streets perpendicular to Main Street. According to Grams, it was the perfect location. Close enough to Main Street to draw in the passersby, but not so close that people would wander in looking for a bathroom. That's how she always put it, anyway. The truth of it came out later. It was her dream to own a bookstore, but she and Gramps didn't have a ton of money to make it happen. He put the down payment on the storefront on Jefferson because it was more affordable. They opened it in December of 1966, just a few years before Mom was born.

Before it was a bookstore, it was a yarn shop, so she named it The Nook and Granny in honor of the granny square blanket the old owners crocheted for her as a welcome present. She even kept a little knitting corner in the back for any of the previous customers who wanted to come in and do their yarn crafts. They did, calling themselves "The Hook Club." They'd usually read the smuttiest romances Grams could find and discuss them while knitting or crocheting. Sometimes I was there when they met. That was an education.

After I was born, Grams liked to joke that the name was fate because she had finally fulfilled her true destiny to be a grandma. But I think her destiny was actually to own the shop. She always seemed at home there. She even smelled like the store when she came home—cinnamon and clove.

Turns out it didn't matter where the shop was. The best thing about River-bend Springs is that the people who live here show up for their own. It was an unwritten rule that no one ever bought books from anywhere but The Nook. Grams could find anything and have it here faster than that giant website that ships things to your door, so there was no need to go elsewhere for reading material. The shop did well enough that Gramps retired early to help her run it. And she employed me all through high school.

It was a special shop. A big part of me hopes it still is.

Bracing myself for the worst, I round the corner. And then I see it—the old-timey vintage sign that hangs over the sidewalk reads *The Nook* in big, script lettering and under it, in smaller, bolder font says *and Granny Bookstore, est. 1966.*

It's still here.

A sigh of relief puffs out from between my lips in a frosty, white cloud. I shimmy my shoulders and start walking faster, excitement taking over me.

The bell over the door rings as I open it, and again as I close it behind me. Even before I get a chance to look around, that sound brings me right back to my childhood. I took that sound for granted, I think. It was never something I came back to in my memories, but now that I hear it again, I'm overtaken by nostalgia pressing so hard on my chest, it's almost hard to breathe through it. Same sign, same door, same bell.

I almost expect to turn around and find Grams there, right behind the counter like she always was when I'd visit the shop after school or on summer weekends after getting ice cream with Liam. I'd run into her arms for a big hug and let her warm scent envelop me. Once I was here, it never mattered what happened outside the shop. All of it was trivial, all of it fixable. Until it wasn't.

But Grams isn't there. Instead, there's a wide-eyed teenage girl behind the counter. Other people mill around, looking at books. One woman with bright red hair picks up a book and smells it, then puts it back down to try another. A couple tries to corral their toddler through the kids' section, though he seems more interested in the bestsellers set out around a small, tinsel tree on the front table.

I wave at the girl behind the counter, but she just stares at me, her big green eyes tracking me as I move about the store. I'd be weirded out by it if I weren't so preoccupied with taking in every little detail of the shop. The oak shelves. The worn, red rug. The Hook Club corner right next to the frosted windows on the side of the building. The multi-paned overhead lamps that cast the whole space in warm, yellow light. The smell of cinnamon and clove.

The offerings have been updated, of course. I wouldn't expect the shop to be peddling the same novels it was selling in the late 90s. But everything else is exactly the same, down to the chalkboard signs that still have Grams's handwriting in permanent chalk marker.

I trace a shaky finger over the letters of one of those signs. I'm unsure if these are replicas or if her hand actually touched them, but tears sting the corners of my eyes. In the deepest corner of my heart, I admit that I had dared to hope this place would still be a bookstore. But never in my wildest dreams did I think it could be the same bookstore.

I'm so fucking happy it is.

The poor girl behind the counter is still staring at me. She must think I've lost my marbles. Turning to her, I give her a small, shaky smile.

"I'm Lo Carson," I say. "My grandmother used to own this store, and it's…" I swallow hard against the emotion threatening to rise from my chest. "It hasn't changed a bit since the last time I was here."

The girl laughs nervously. "It's definitely vintage."

Walking around and running my hands over the edges of the bookshelves, I keep taking in every detail. The chip in the wood from when I ran my huge backpack into the shelf on accident. The worn armchair I used to snuggle up in next to Grams as I told her about my day. The back corner where Liam found me once, delirious with a fever and insistent that I keep the shop open because Grams trusted me. He closed the shop, carried me to his truck, and drove me home. He was so worried about me that he stayed in my room that night and read a book on the floor next to my bed.

I probably should have known then how he felt about me. If only I did, then I could have seen all of it coming. Maybe if I had been prepared, I could have responded better. Or I might have had the chance to realize how in love with him I was, too.

Hindsight is twenty-twenty, I guess.

"Who owns this place now?" I ask, still trying to drink everything in and store it up for later. Now that I remember how much I've missed this place, I don't want a single scratch or decoration to escape my memory. "Why didn't they change anything?"

"Um…" The girl shifts awkwardly on her feet. "I don't really know?"

The upspeak gets my attention. I narrow my eyes skeptically. "You don't know why they didn't change anything, or you don't know who you work for?"

"Both?" She smiles innocently, but she shoves her hands deeper into her pockets, most likely to keep them from trembling.

"How can you not know who owns this place? Surely someone signs your paychecks."

"Oh, no." She lets out a breathy laugh. "I have direct deposit."

"It was a figure of speech."

The girl sighs, then mutters something under her breath. She looks like she's fighting an internal war with herself, but her common sense must win because she slumps her shoulders and gives me a pointed look. "Listen, I make minimum wage and I'm not really sure what is going on around here, but I promised I wouldn't say anything, and I'm not a snitch so..." She shrugs.

"Promised who?"

She opens her mouth as if to respond, then closes it again. "Nice try. But, uh...feel free to look around." Her eyes dart toward the other side of the shop, but she lowers them quickly and then excuses herself to the back room.

That was strange. Quickly, I walk to the other side of the shop where she clearly didn't mean to look. It only takes a few seconds to find what she was indicating. To anyone else, it'd look like an innocent Christmas decoration. But I know better, because in the corner of the display set up on the table is a nutcracker. This one is shaped like a snowman, and it's actually kind of cute.

Why couldn't Grams have sent this one to my apartment instead of that nightmare fuel?

Looking around to make sure no one is paying attention to me, I pick up the nutcracker and flip it over. Sure enough, an envelope with my name on it is taped to the bottom. I carefully detach it and open it up to find another letter in Grams's scrawling handwriting.

---

*My Dear Gloria,*

*Finally. You finally made it. But your job here isn't done. Stay a while. Make yourself at home, if you will. Your destiny awaits.*

*Ha ha ha. That was a little dramatic. I couldn't help myself. Seriously though, you know as well as I do that you're not done here. Buckle up, buttercup. You have more secrets to uncover.*

*Love you forever,*

*Grams*

---

I try not to slam the nutcracker back down on the table in frustration. What does she mean my job isn't done? I did what she asked—I came to check on the shop. What more does she want from me?

But if I know Grams, leaving now would only cause more chaos back home until I finally uncover whatever it is she wants me to find. So now I'm stuck here at least one more night while I ponder the riddles of the ghost of Christmas past.

At least I have heat this time, I guess.

I skim the letter again, and my eyes snag on one line. *Make yourself at home, if you will.*

"Dammit, Grams," I hiss. "You *wanted* me in that house, didn't you? Ugh, *why*?"

I don't really expect an answer, but I wait for one anyway, just in case. Nothing comes. Because that would be too easy.

Clutching the letter in my coat pocket, I quickly exit the shop, ducking my head against the cold that greets me as soon as I open the door. And because I'm not looking, I slam right into the chest of someone walking by.

No, not just someone. Liam.

I'm happy to find out that he does still smell like warm spices, and his chest is still the perfect height to bury myself in.

Only, I can't do that. That would be inappropriate. So I take a step back.

"Sorry!" I exclaim. "Sorry, sorry, sorry. I wasn't watching where I was going."

"It's really okay," he says softly, his voice infused with sincerity. "Everything all right?"

"Um..." My gaze trails up his hardened chest, over the dark stubble on his neck—that's new, and I'm not quite ready to think about what it does to my insides—and to his dark brown eyes. He looks down at me with concern etched into his features. And suddenly I want nothing else but to move back into his body and let it fold around me.

Shaking my head as if to clear it, I take another step backward so I don't embarrass myself. "Yeah. Sort of? I don't know." I hitch a thumb over my shoulder. "I'm thrown off. Did you know The Nook looks exactly the same as it did when we were kids?"

"Of course he knows," Mia pipes up. I hadn't noticed her there. "That's our favorite bookstore."

Liam frowns down at her, but I study him intensely. He still comes here? And he brings his kid? Why? And why didn't he mention it this morning when I said I needed to check in on the place?

When he meets my gaze again, it's with a scowl. I'm not sure what that's all about, but I know from past experience that I can wait him out and eventually he'll talk.

"It's the only place for books in town," he grumbles.

"But doesn't it remind you of—" I start.

"You," he cuts me off gruffly. But then, he softens and his scowl disappears. "Yes."

My mouth suddenly goes dry, and my breath hitches. "Oh."

We stand there awkwardly for another moment, neither of us seeming to know what to say, until Mia loudly and very conspicuously clears her throat. When Liam doesn't respond to her, she throws her whole body into his leg to get his attention. He looks down at her, and she clears her throat again, widening her eyes.

"Oh. Right." He directs his attention to me. "The Christmas Market is tonight. I know you said you were leaving, but..." He shrugs stiffly.

The letter in my hand feels weightier than it should all of a sudden. I can almost hear the words in Grams's voice: *You know as well as I do that you're not done here.*

*All right, Grams. You win this round,* I think. Whatever she wants can't have anything to do with Liam. I'm sure she's only interested in the shop. But I'm here for another night anyway, and I can't resist the Christmas Market. I never could.

"Turns out I'm sticking around for a little longer than I planned," I say.

It's hard to tell, but I think Liam cracks a hint of a smile. "Great. Pick you up at six?"

# Chapter 9

## Liam

When the Christmas Market started downtown back in the 50s, it was just the local shops setting up tents outside and encouraging people to walk around and spend some extra money. It grew from there, with restaurants on the outskirts of town coming in to sell special holiday food and a tent in one of the parks where people could sit and eat. A few years later came the beer garden, and then it was exponential. Vendors from outside Riverbend Springs wanted in on the action. By the time Lo and I were old enough to go on our own, the town had to start taking applications, and they were able to charge fees for anyone who didn't run a local business. Now, the entire event pays for most of the town's other programs throughout the year.

It is absolutely magical. Main Street and several of the side streets are completely shut down. Red and green tents line the walkways, and every booth is decked out in Christmas lights and décor. With the snow already covering the ground and starting to come down again in small, delicate flurries, it looks like something out of one of Mia's picture books.

As we join the throng of people walking toward downtown with Mia's mittened hand in mine and Lo walking close on the other side of her, I try not to let my heart get carried away. Which lasts about five minutes before I decide it's too much effort. This is what I always wanted but never dared to hope for—spending time with my little family, enjoying the twinkle lights and hot chocolate, then snuggling into a warm bed at home.

Maybe I can let myself pretend just for tonight. What's the harm in that?

"Where should we go first?" Mia is practically jumping the whole way to Main Street. "Ornament decorating? Candy Cane Lane? Ahh!" She screams, then she does jump up and down, pointing somewhere in the distance. "Is that a giant nutcracker? Dad! Come on! Take my picture!"

She sidles up to the nutcracker, which is at least twice her size, and clasps her hands primly in front of her as she tilts her head with a wide, cheesy grin. I fumble as I take my phone out of my pocket to snap a few pictures, hoping to get one with her eyes open. Lo stiffens a bit beside me and mumbles something.

"What was that?" I ask her.

"Hm?" She blinks rapidly. "Oh, nothing." But she's still frowning deeply as Mia comes back to my side.

I want to reach out and run my finger down the arch of her nose like I used to, but I hold myself back. "You got a vendetta against nutcrackers or something?"

"Something like that."

Her vehemence is so unexpected that I can't help but laugh. Luckily, that breaks her scowl into a smile. We stand there, people moving around us and Mia's hand warm in mine again. But all I can see is Lo, those light brown eyes, her hair curling out under that ridiculous hat that her mom must have made for her, the lights out of focus behind her.

It's like I'm watching a movie, and she's the star.

"Daddy! Daddy!" Mia starts jumping up and down again. "It's Jesse!"

Sure enough, when I come to my senses, Jesse is sauntering toward us with purpose, clearly stifling a grin.

"Imagine seeing you here." He cocks one of his fair eyebrows at me, then his blue eyes slide to Lo. "Good to see you again, Lo."

"You too, Jesse."

He glances back at me, and I can practically see the gears turning in his brain. Then, he gets down on one knee to look Mia in the eye. "Did you know that there are actual reindeer in the park this year?"

She gasps, eyes like saucers, as she practically vibrates with childlike energy. "Oh, this I have to see." Tugging on my arm, she looks up at me. "Daddy, can we go?"

"You know what?" Jesse says before I can answer. "Why don't I take you? I imagine your dad and Lo have some catching up to do." He winks at her.

Her excitement tempers itself into a sly look. She nods slowly. "Good idea," she says, then turns her face up to me. "Remember what we talked about."

Then, she transfers her hand to Jesse's and they're gone.

"What the hell was that about?" Lo asks as we watch them skip off into the distance.

"I think my daughter and my friend are conspiring, but I'm not sure to what end."

Lo giggles, the sound of it so bright that my body turns on its own to face her. Like I'm a sunflower and she's the sun.

"Sounded like they wanted us to be alone," she says suggestively.

I shake my head. "Mia doesn't know what that means." I pause, considering what to say next. "But full disclosure, she has made it her mission to ensure you are not alone on Christmas."

"That's..." Lo trails off, looking in the direction they went. I fully expect her to finish that sentence with *not happening*, but she says, "really sweet. She's a great kid."

The feeling that rises in me is one I haven't felt in a while. It feels a lot like hope.

"She's the best," I say with pride. "Even if she is a little conspirator."

Lo laughs again. "So, what do you want to do?"

"Same thing we always do," I say with ease. "Fifteen minutes to find the perfect gift. Under twenty-five dollars. And, go!" I jog off.

"What? No! I'm not prepared for this. You have an unfair head start!"

"Keep griping and you'll never find one," I call over my shoulder.

But she's right. I do have an unfair advantage. As a business owner, I had a preview of the vendors coming this year, so I know exactly where I'm going. I find the booth right away, consider which option I want for all of five minutes, then make my purchase.

For a moment after I step out of the tent, I don't know where to go next. We always used to meet at the hot chocolate tent, but we didn't say where to exchange gifts this year, so I wonder if she'll go back to our starting point.

Ultimately, I decide tradition wins and make my way to the hot chocolate tent.

She's waiting there for me, her arms crossed and a bag dangling from one of her hands. "Do I win any points for speed?"

"Depends." I tip my chin in the direction of her bag. "Whatcha got?"

She shakes her head. "This was your idea. You first."

Suddenly, embarrassment washes over me. I should have gone with something safer—thought less with my heart and more with my head. But it's too late now, so I hand the bag over.

Lo eyes me warily before peeking in the bag. Her jaw drops as she pulls out a crystal star, the panes sparkling in the lights. I reach over and press a switch, lighting it up from the inside. It throws tiny rainbow sparkles over the features of her face, somehow making her even more beautiful.

"Oh wow," she breathes. "It's really pretty." She studies it for a moment longer, then raises her gaze to me in question.

"It's for the top of a Christmas tree," I explain, growing more uncomfortable with each word. "But you... I don't know. You reminded me of a star earlier. One day back and somehow, you've lit us up again." I shake my head, frustrated at my ability to find the right words. "I'm sorry. It's stupid. I'll take it back."

I reach out my hand for her to give it to me, but she clutches it to her chest.

"Are you kidding me? No way. I love it." Her smile is even brighter than the star. Brighter than all the lights surrounding us. Guiding me to her like she always did.

But then she grimaces. "Okay, but mine is actually stupid. I wasn't sure if we were going for nostalgia or something safe or..." She shrugs helplessly. "I went for funny."

"Oh, I can't want to see this." I make a gimme motion with my fingers. "Hand it over."

Reluctantly, she holds out the bag. I snatch it from her before she can change her mind and reach inside to pull out...

"A toilet ornament?"

Lo presses her mouth into a straight line, then rolls her eyes in exasperation. "I figured without Maisey's toilet problem, we probably never would have talked again."

I roll my lips together and press down on them with my teeth. My cheeks puff out with repressed laughter.

"I did the best I could with fifteen minutes. After fourteen years apart, no less." She throws her arms up and lets them smack at her sides. "I'm sorry. You gave me this heartfelt gift, and I gave you a toilet."

The way she says it—full of so much defeat—has me howling with laughter. Her nostrils flare in frustration, but I can tell she's hiding a smile.

"It's perfect. I'll cherish it forever," I assure her.

"Please don't."

"It'll have a special place on the tree every year. Right where everyone can see it."

"Put it on the back of the tree, at least."

"And I'll tell everyone about how my long-lost best friend came back after fourteen years and bought me a toilet because it reminded her of me."

"I..." She trails off and her expression falls into something pained. "I'm sorry I left."

I told myself I wasn't going to bring it up unless she did. What's done is done. But here she is, apologizing for it all as snowflakes stick to her long eyelashes and her cheeks turn pink with cold. And I can't let her do that.

"You didn't do anything wrong," I say gently. "I…" Again, I'm at a loss for words. "I always loved you, Lo. You were my best friend." God, that's a scary thing to say aloud again, but there's no use denying it. "You weren't ready for more. I shouldn't have pushed it."

She shakes her head slowly, tears gathering at the corners of her eyes. I have to resist the urge to reach out and brush them away. "We both have regrets."

That feeling of hope starts building even bigger in me, but I shove it down. I can't let myself hope for what I really want. It's too soon. Too irrational. Even for Christmas.

I fold her into my arms. She buries her face in my chest and inhales deeply, just like she used to. "We're here now," I tell her, rubbing her back. "I vote we move forward, not backward."

"Sounds good to me." She tips her face up to mine, and I'm struck with the urge to capture her lips with mine. Maybe now that we've cleared the air, we could—

"Okay, but I have to know." She interrupts my train of thought. "Who owns The Nook, and why did they keep it exactly the same?"

I open my mouth to respond, but a tiny body crashes into my leg with a grunt. Lo steps back quickly, and I immediately miss her body next to mine.

"Hot chocolate time!" Mia clenches her fists and yells into the night sky. Snowflakes dot her cheeks.

"How much sugar has Jesse given you?" I ask.

"Way too much," he says as he approaches. "You know I can't resist her."

She clasps her mittened hands together under her chin and bats her eyelashes at me. "What's a little more? It's almost Christmas!"

I narrow my eyes at Jesse, who shrugs. But before I can say anything about it, Mia grabs Lo's hand and tugs her to get in line. It hits me then, that these are my girls holding hands, waiting for hot chocolate. Or, at least, I want them to be.

Jesse claps me on the shoulder. "You're in trouble."

"Yep," I say simply.

He chuckles. "Good luck, man." Then, after some consideration, he adds, "I think it might end better this time."

I don't know what gives him that impression, but I really hope he's right.

# Chapter 10

## Lo

WHEN I WAKE UP, I have even more questions than I fell asleep with. There were about three different times when I was sure Liam was going to kiss me last night, the last of which being when he dropped me off. I'm pretty sure he would have too, if Mia weren't pretending to be asleep in the back of his truck.

And I'd be lying if I said I hadn't wanted him to.

But there's nothing I can do about that right now short of going to his house and throwing myself at him. Probably not the best idea given that he has his daughter with him this week, and I don't actually know where he lives now.

I opt instead to deal with the Grams situation. The girl who worked at the shop was weirdly evasive, which makes me more curious about who owns the place and why they haven't changed anything about it in over a decade. Is it a town nostalgia thing? Does it still make money? I have so many questions.

Since I'm nice and toasty warm this morning, I start by checking out the kitchen to see if it's fully stocked like the rest of the house. No luck. Not even a coffee bean to suck on. So I shower, make myself presentable, and head over to the diner.

One of the perks—and drawbacks—of being a teacher is that I'm an early riser even on days when I don't have school. It's still early when I get there, so it's pretty empty. I snag a booth near the front and pretend to look at the menu, but I already know I can't turn down those holly jolly waffles.

"Well, hey there." Instead of taking my order, Jesse sits across from me in the booth, a sly grin on his face. "How was the rest of your evening?"

"Great," I say slowly, narrowing my eyes. "How about you?"

"Nothing special." He clasps his hands in front of him on the table. "So, let's cut to the chase. What are your intentions with my friend?"

I rear back, surprised. "Oh, we're going to do this, now?"

"You broke his heart when you left." Jesse shoots me a pointed look. "If you're going to leave again, I'd prefer you did it before you two get all hot and heavy."

"Ew." I grimace. "No one says that."

"I say that."

"You shouldn't." I sigh, unwilling to have this conversation with him but seeing no way out of it. "He broke my heart too, you know."

Jesse eyes me skeptically. "He put his heart out there and you rejected it." He raises his hands, palms out. "I'm not suggesting you should have started something with him you weren't ready for, but that was a pretty vulnerable thing for an eighteen-year-old to do. And I'm definitely not suggesting you start something with him now, but if you're going to leave again, maybe just be upfront about it." He looks over his shoulder, then leans in, lowering his voice. "Liam has developed a gruff exterior, but he's a big softie on the inside. Don't tell anyone I told you."

I cock an eyebrow. "Your secret's safe with me."

Jesse hits the table softly with an open palm. "Good talk. You want the waffles again?"

"Absolutely."

He pushes himself to standing, but before he can move away, I say, "Hey, I have a question for you actually. Who owns The Nook now?"

Regarding me strangely, he taps his fingers against the side of his pants. "Why do you want to know?"

"It's the reason I'm here. Grams...well..." I clear my throat. No way am I going to get into the whole backstory. "I was there yesterday, and it was like I took a time machine back to the early aughts. I'm curious, is all."

He tilts his head, and the drumming of his fingertips on his leg stops. "You don't know?"

"Should I?" I raise my eyebrows in question.

Chuckling softly, he rubs his palm against his jawline and shakes his head slowly. "Oh, man. I can't tell you that."

"But you know."

He nods, then makes a zipping motion over his lips.

"Jesse," I plead. "Come on. What's the big deal? Just tell me."

"Mm-mmm." He shakes his head again. "But if you're searching for answers about that, I'd suggest going back there"—he checks his watch—"sometime in the next two hours. I'll grab you those waffles." He turns to walk to the counter.

First the girl at the shop, now Jesse. "What the hell is going on around here? Why won't anyone tell me?" This is the weirdest fucking thing that has ever happened to me. It's such a strange secret to keep. And the fact that Grams has been haunting me about it the cherry on top.

"It won't be a secret forever, Lo. Trust me on this one."

"I don't trust you to do anything but make waffles," I grumble.

Jesse must hear me because he laughs again. I'm glad someone is getting some joy out of this. But now I'm annoyed enough that I'm going to march myself right over to The Nook and demand answers.

Right after I finish those waffles.

***

This time when I walk into The Nook, I'm ready for it. I'm not going to be snowed by the nostalgia this time. I'm here for answers. No nutcrackers, sentimental details, or teenaged employees are going to get in my way.

As soon as the door closes behind me, I look for someone who I can harass with my questions, but there's nobody there. That's not unheard of if there's only one person working and they're in the back doing inventory or something. Especially if it's that teenager again—I bet she has her headphones on and didn't hear the bell.

I wait up front for a few minutes but quickly grow impatient. "I don't have all day," I mutter to myself. What if I were an actual customer? They'd have lost a sale by now.

Good thing I'm not a customer, though. I know exactly where to find that kid, so I stomp across the shop and through the narrow hallway marked *Employees Only*.

Former employees count. Probably.

Only, there's no one back here. I look in the back room where my favorite beanbag chairs still sit. There's a stuffed dog and a stack of early reader books back here, which tells me it's been used by a child recently. My heart squeezes knowing someone else is appreciating this space the way I used to.

No. I told myself I wasn't going to get emotional, I was going to get answers. *You can gush about how cute this is later*, I tell myself as I walk past the back room and round the corner into the office. The light is on, so someone must have been here, but it's also unoccupied at the moment. I remember Grams making phone calls and doing her financial stuff back here. It's a tiny space with the same desk taking up almost the entire wall. Stacks of books—some of which look way older than me—are piled up from the floor, but the desk is clear save for one paper sitting in the middle of it.

Since there's no one here, I let my curiosity get the best of me. I pick the paper up, surprised to see Grams's handwriting.

> *This Agreement is made on December 1, 20XX between Gloria Leigh Carson ('Seller') and Liam Jonathan White ('Buyer'). Seller agrees to sell, and Buyer agrees to purchase, the Business operating under the name 'The*

> *Nook and Granny Bookstore', located at 109 Jefferson Avenue, Riverbend Springs, Iowa, including all tangible and intangible assets as described in Schedule A.*
>
> *The total purchase price for the Business is $1. The sale includes all assets listed in Schedule A, which includes all furniture, books, other for sale items, point of sale system, and anything else currently in the store.*
>
> *All business liabilities, including but not limited to debts, taxes, and lawsuits, shall remain the sole responsibility of the Seller, unless otherwise specified in this Agreement.*
>
> *Upon sale of the Business, Buyer agrees to sell the Business to Gloria Lauren Carson, granddaughter of Gloria Leigh Carson, for $1 should she ever want to purchase the Business.*
>
> *Gloria Leigh Carson*
> *Seller*
>
> *Liam Jonathan White*
> *Buyer*

It takes me three times reading through the contract before I fully understand what I'm seeing. Even then, I'm at a loss for words. All I can do is stare at the paper until I hear heavy footsteps in the doorway.

"Lo?" Liam asks. "What are you doing here?"

Tearing my gaze away from the paper, I look at him. He's wearing another lined flannel over a T-shirt and jeans, but no hat today. His black hair is mussed, and his dark eyebrows are pulled together. The stubble on his jaw catches the light, and I idly wonder what it might feel like to have it scrape against my skin.

It occurs to me then exactly how much I missed by staying away for so long. He's fully a man now—his shoulders broader, his muscles more toned. And he's been here, running this shop, keeping it exactly the way Grams wanted it.

For me.

"You—" I'm cut off by the lump of emotion in my throat. "You."

It's the only word I can get out. The only one that matters.

It's him. It's always been him. I was just too scared and stubborn to see it.

Luckily, I don't have to think of any more words because Liam crosses the tiny office in two long strides, wraps me in his arms, and kisses me.

# Chapter 11

## Lo

THE KISS IS EVERYTHING I never knew I wanted. Scratch that. I always knew I wanted it—I was just too afraid to admit it. Liam tastes like mint and chocolate, and his lips are warm and soft. And when his tongue gently asks for entry, I'm helpless to stop the little moan that escapes me. He captures that moan and he grips the back of my coat, pulling me nearer. But there are far too many layers of fabric between us. I want to fold myself into him, feel his hard edges meet my soft ones, explore everything I've been missing and more.

The sound of the shop bell has us leaping apart. We're breathless, like two teenagers caught making out in the back rooms. I suppose we were making out in the back rooms, but we're not teenagers. Not anymore.

Briefly, I think that the fact that we're grown adults means I can keep kissing him if I want to. And I do want to. But before I can pull him to me again, he smirks, regarding me with that dark intensity he always had but somehow darker now. Full of promise.

I shiver, which only makes his smirk grow.

"That'll be Kate," he says.

Blinking rapidly, I try to tell myself to snap out of it. "Who's Kate?"

"The girl who works here. You met her yesterday."

"Oh." That's right. Someone entered the shop. That's why I'm not kissing him anymore. I really need to get it together. "The one who wouldn't answer any of my questions. That was not helpful. You might want to talk to *your employee* about that."

Liam's smile turns indulgent, dripping with sweetness. Not once does his gaze leave mine, and I can't say I want it to.

"She was just doing what I asked. I wanted to tell you myself." He nods, indicating the paper I'm now realizing is still clutched in my hand. "I came in here this morning to pull that out and show you. I was going to find you. I had a whole plan."

Carefully, I lay the paper down on the desk and smooth it out. "I'm sorry. I didn't mean to ruin your plan. I'll just pretend I was never here—"

He cuts me off by grabbing me by the waist and pressing another kiss to my lips. This one is more chaste than the last, but my toes curl anyway.

"You're a snoop," he says as he brushes his nose against mine.

"There wasn't anyone out front. Bad for business, really."

"Oh, look at you. A business owner already."

*Upon sale of the Business, Buyer agrees to sell the Business to Gloria Lauren Carson, granddaughter of Gloria Leigh Carson, for $1 should she ever want to purchase the Business.*

That's what the contract said. That this place is mine. Grams had Liam keep it for me. And that's why she wanted me here to check in on the place. My place.

"The bookstore is mine," I whisper.

"If you want it." His deep voice rumbles through me, and I can't think past wanting *him*, let alone a whole store.

"You kept it for me," I say with awe.

"If you want it," he repeats. "That's kind of an important part of the contract. No one is forcing you into anything. It's a decision you'll have to make for yourself."

Footsteps coming nearer have us reluctantly stepping apart again.

"We should probably talk about this?" I raise my eyebrows in question. It's true—we should—but it's really a thinly veiled invitation to see him later.

He nods. "Mia is at a friend's for a playdate today. Something about a Christmas movie pajama party?" Shrugging, he huffs a laugh. "I don't know, but she was really excited about it."

"Are you jealous?" I tease. "We could have our own Christmas movie pajama party if you want."

Almost tentatively, he reaches out and runs a fingertip down my nose. He always used to do that. I had forgotten, but the memory swells in me, warms me from the inside out. It's such a tender motion. It probably always was, but I was too young to see it.

He loved me.

Maybe he still could.

"That doesn't sound terrible, actually," he says. "But no, I was thinking I could make you dinner?"

I gasp playfully. "He owns a company. He owns a *business*. And he cooks?"

Liam's low chuckle is music to my ears. "I have a kid. It's kind of a necessity."

"So what you're telling me is you'll make me some chicken nuggets and boxed mac 'n cheese?"

"If that's what you want." He brushes my nose again, and I just about melt all the way into a puddle.

"If I wanted girl dinner, I'd go back to my lonely apartment and cook for myself." I let out a little self-deprecating laugh. "I expect to be impressed."

"I can be impressive." As if he can't get enough of me, he kisses me again. And I'm pretty sure that, yes, he can be impressive. In a lot of ways.

"Come over around four," he says. "I'll text you my address."

***

Liam's house is about ten minutes outside of town, and when I pull into his long driveway, I can see why. A grove of giant, snow-covered pine trees is the backdrop for the A-frame mountain cabin complete with wood siding and dark accents. It's Iowa, though, so there are no mountains, but it doesn't seem to matter. It's quiet here—nary a neighbor in sight. Knowing Liam, that was probably by design.

The house is massive. I had no idea construction paid so well. Suddenly, the bottle of wine I picked up on my way over here feels completely inadequate. Alas, it'll have to do.

I tread carefully as I walk up to the front door. Everything is plowed and salted with obvious care, but it's starting to snow pretty hard again, and the last thing I need is to wipe out on my ass before I even get inside. When I ring the doorbell, it takes a few moments for him to answer the door. He's flushed and a bit out of breath.

"You're on time."

"You said four." I check my watch. "It's four."

"Right. I just…" He shakes his head quickly. "Never mind. Come in."

He opens the door wider, and I brush past him and into the front room. It is just as huge as the outside would suggest. The vaulted ceiling reaches up at least twenty feet high. A gorgeous chandelier casts the space in warm light. To the right is a dining room furnished with a long, dark table dotted with poinsettias in vases. In the window is a Christmas tree adorned with sparkling gold and silver orbs.

Liam takes my coat and gives me a moment to take in the space, then leads me through a small hallway to the kitchen and living room. Winter-white cabinets surround the kitchen space contrasting the dark countertops and stainless-steel appliances. In the middle of the kitchen is a huge island that houses the stove. The whole space is open to the living room where a fire is roaring in the fireplace and another tree is lit with rainbow lights and decorated with clearly handmade and meaningful ornaments.

As I gape at the space, Liam gently pries the bottle of wine from my hand. He walks over to the island and opens the door to a wine fridge in the side of it—a wine fridge! And somehow, that's the detail that sends me over the edge.

"What the fuck, Liam?"

He looks at me quizzically. "What?"

I stretch my arms wide because I can do that and not touch the walls like I can in my apartment. "This place! You actually live here? Like, this is *yours*?"

His low laugh echoes off the cavernous walls. Okay, not really, but it could. That's how huge this place is.

"Is it"—he winks—"impressive?"

"Fuck yes, it is. How the hell did you do this?"

He shrugs, and that's when I finally take stock of him. He's wearing a forest green T-shirt and dark jeans, a step up from the more casual work clothes I've seen him in thus far. It's pretty obvious that he ran a comb through his hair, too, which is so cute I can hardly stand it. He's not wearing any socks, and he doesn't need to because...

"Are your floors heated?" I exclaim, looking down at my feet.

He tips his head back and laughs heartily. "They are."

"Oh my god. I'm going to need a glass of wine and an explanation. In that order."

Smiling to himself, he pours me a glass from the bottle of red that's open on the counter. He hands it to me, and I take a healthy gulp.

"There's not much to explain. I went to college, majored in civil engineering, and decided I didn't want to work for anyone else so I started my own company." He shrugs. "And yeah, I do well, but it helps to know people in the industry when you're building a house."

I look around the space with a new appreciation. "You built this place?"

"Designed and built, yes."

"Wow." Nodding with a heaping dose of respect, I take another sip of my wine. "Okay. I'm officially impressed."

"Good, because I'm actually making you boxed mac 'n cheese."

"The house makes up for it," I tell him, then reconsider. "Wait, really?"

"No," he says with laughter. "Steak with a red wine reduction sauce and fingerling potatoes. I remember how you used to order red meat every time you went out because you knew all your mom had at home was tofu."

Just when I thought my heart couldn't grow any bigger, it does. "Liam—" I'm choked with emotion and can't get any more words out.

He takes my wine glass from me and sets it gently on the counter, then returns his hand to cup the back of my neck. His thumb grazes lightly over my cheek.

"If I start kissing you right now, I won't stop."

"Okay." I'm not surprised to find that I'm breathless.

Shaking his head, he settles for a kiss on my nose. "You came for dinner and a story."

"I didn't not come for kisses," I grumble, annoyed.

"Later," he promises. "Sit. I'll cook and talk and then...we can see what happens."

# Chapter 12

## Liam

Lo is gorgeous. Her whiskey eyes and brown hair practically glow in the light of the kitchen. As she sits at the island with the Christmas tree behind her and the snow coming down outside, it's like the perfect Christmas present has found me.

I vow silently not to take it for granted. Even if she won't stay, if she doesn't want any of this, I have her for now. That'll have to be enough.

Setting a pan on the stove, I warm some butter and then put the steaks on to cook. She watches me and waits, sipping her wine every so often. She's so beautiful, I can hardly stand it. It takes all my willpower to do as I said and not kiss her.

"I was home on break my senior year of college," I begin. Lo leans forward on her elbows, an active listener. "Your Grams cornered me. Told me she was going to will me her shop. She was afraid that if she willed it to you, you'd sell it without thinking about it too much. I told her she was crazy, that you loved that shop and you'd never do such a thing, but she insisted that you were too stubborn to see past your own bullheadedness, and you'd have sold it out of spite."

Lo makes a face, considering. "Four years ago, she'd probably have been right."

"I came to the same conclusion."

Her jaw drops, and her hand flies to her heart in mock offense. "How dare you."

"Anyway," I continue as I move the steaks to a platter to rest and add the aromatics to the pan. "The plan was always for you to have the shop. I'm only the intermediary. But I refused to have her will it to me, so she let me buy it." I huff a laugh at the memory. "I spent a week in and out of the bank, trying to figure out how much money I could put down and how much of a loan I could take out."

"You did all that on the off chance that I'd come to my senses?"

"Yeah," I say as if it was the simplest decision in the world. Because it was. But I shrug it off. "It was a good business decision, too. At the time, I already knew I didn't want to work for anyone else. I had plans to start my own construction company, and I figured I could use the collateral from the shop to help me with that. It was a win-win."

She purses her lips against a smile. "Smart."

"Well, yeah, until your Grams came to me with that contract." I add the red wine to the pan and let it reduce. "She wouldn't hear of negotiating anything differently, so I had to go to the diner to break a ten for the dollar to give her. She basically continued to run the shop while I finished school, and well into those first years while I started my company. She kept sixty percent of the profits and called it her payment for the shop but better because she wasn't charging me interest."

Lo laughs and rolls her eyes. "Sounds like Grams." She finishes off her wine. I refill her glass and pour one for myself. She takes another sip, humming. "What would you do with the shop if I didn't want it?"

"I'll admit that I wouldn't let myself consider the possibility." I set out two plates, forks, and steak knives. "But now, Mia loves it. The town is still fiercely loyal, so the place practically runs itself. We're in the black every month, even if it's narrow. I'd probably give it to her eventually." I eye her over my glass of wine as I take a drink. "Are you saying you don't want it?"

"No," she says quickly. "But... I have to think about it. Is that okay?"

I take the potatoes out of the oven and slice the steak. "Take all the time you need." Using the excuse of plating the food so I don't have to look at her, I say cautiously, "Maybe you should stay here until after Christmas while you consider everything."

"Did Mia put you up to that?" she jokes, but I can tell there's an edge to it. Like she wants it to be coming from me.

"It'd make her very happy," I admit, raising my gaze to meet hers as I set a plate in front of her. "But it'd make me happy, too."

She makes a show of thinking about it, which makes both of us laugh. "I guess I could clear my schedule."

I come around the island with my plate and sit next to her. "Good."

We eat for a little while in silence. Lo gazes out the kitchen window, lost in thought. I'm not about to interrupt her with some useless small talk.

"It's really coming down out there," she remarks.

"Mmm," I hum as I swallow my bite. "You probably shouldn't drive. You know those country roads aren't plowed."

She regards me with mock skepticism. "Just looking out for me, I'm sure."

"Always."

Softening, she forks one last potato, then stands. "Are you going to give me the tour or what?"

I can't tell her no. I never could. So we take our wine glasses with as I show her the rest of the house. The living room, Mia's princess bedroom, and when we get to my bedroom, Lo doesn't hesitate to step inside for a better look. She stops short when she sees the cabinet where I display all my baseball hats, many of them collector's items from my favorite teams.

"Woah, that's a lot of hats," she says, her eyes growing wide.

"Impressive?" I ask.

She gives a short, staccato laugh as she tucks a piece of hair behind her ear. "Sure." She scans the rows of hats. "And not a single red one in sight."

"Not my color," I tell her. I've never gone for the bright, obvious ones.

"Not even a Santa hat?"

"Do I look like the kind of person who would wear a Santa hat to you?"

Turning to fully face me, she drags her gaze down my body and takes her time on her way back up again. Suddenly it's too warm in here, and all I can think about is whether or not she likes what she sees.

"I bet you would if I asked really nicely." She raises her eyebrows suggestively.

Just when I'm about to throw her on the bed and have my way with her, my phone rings. Groaning, I pull it out of my pocket. When I see the name, I glance at Lo apologetically before answering.

"Hello?"

"Hi, Liam. It's Heather."

"Everything okay with the girls?"

"Yeah, they're great, but the snow is going to make it hard to drive. The girls are begging for a sleepover. I don't mind, and I'd rather not be out in this."

Lo is studying me with concern, but all I can think is that this is the best Christmas gift ever—she's here, and Mia is safe with a family we've known forever. I excuse myself into another room and ask to talk to her. I make sure she wants to stay. (She really, really does). I remind her of the rules. (She knows.) I tell her to say thank you to Miss Heather for having her. (She yells it so loudly that I have to move the phone away from my ear.) And I remind her that I'll brave the snow or any weather to come get her if she wants to come home. (She gives me the five-going-on-fifteen exasperation that this will not be happening.)

When I hang up and come back into the bedroom, Lo is still there. Her empty wine glass is sitting on top of the dresser, and her arms are folded as her gaze meets mine.

"It's kind of weird to hear you in dad mode," she says.

"Bad weird?"

"No," she shakes her head. "Just different."

I can't keep myself from touching her any longer. I set my wine glass down next to hers and cross the room to draw her into me. She tips her head up to meet my gaze, and I bow to her, my lips finally meeting hers. Her hands bunch around the fabric of my shirt, and I grip the back of her head, angling her exactly where I want her. Our tongues dance together, the flavor of wine mingling with something so distinctly her. And I find myself wondering what she tastes like elsewhere.

"Mia is staying at her friend's house." I pull myself away long enough to tell her, then press a line of kisses down her neck. She moans, gripping me tighter. "The snow is bad. You really should stay here."

"Convenient," she says sarcastically.

I lightly graze my teeth over the sensitive skin where her neck meets her collarbone, and she gasps.

"Do that again and I'll stay as long as you want," she whispers.

Meeting her gaze, I try to read everything I can in those whiskey brown eyes. "Are you okay with this? Really?"

"If you're asking if I want to sleep with you, Liam, the answer is an emphatic yes."

That's all I need to hear. I pick her up at her waist and toss her on the bed. She squeals and giggles until I lift her shirt over her head to expose a red satin bra. My cock strains against my jeans.

"Festive," I comment.

"I'll admit I had some hopes of my own for tonight." She drags her bottom lip through her teeth. "Your turn."

Practically growling, I fist the back of my shirt and pull it over my head. Her wide eyes drink me in, and I let her. Based on the pink tint of her cheeks, I think she likes what she sees.

Unable to wait another minute, I kiss and lick my way from her chin to her breasts. I pull aside the satin cup of her bra to draw a nipple into my mouth. She squirms underneath me, her hands grappling with the fly of my jeans. I tease her other nipple with my fingers as she finally pulls me free. Her hand circles around my cock and she pumps a few times. It feels so good, I almost collapse onto her.

"Fuck, Lo," I moan. "I've waited so long for this."

She captures my lips in a silent answer. The kiss is so tender, so sweet, and I dare to hope that maybe she's been waiting, too.

It doesn't take long for us to grow heated again, and I wiggle free of my jeans and boxers. I make quick work of her pants, too. She lays there, open for me, biting her lip and daring me with her eyes to take everything I've ever wanted.

So I do. Dipping my head between her gorgeous thighs, I lick up her seam, lapping up every drop of her I can get. When I reach her clit, she cries out and brings her knees up, clutching the skin behind her legs.

"Liam. Oh my god."

Her hips buck into me, so I place a heavy palm over her abdomen to keep her exactly where I want her. I lick and suck and savor her. Her moans become breathy as her legs start to shake. I press a finger inside her so I can feel her clench around it, and that's all it takes to send her over the edge. She comes with my name on her lips, making my dick rock hard.

I watch her come down as I kneel, lightly circling my hand around myself. She's so fucking beautiful with her hair strewn over the pillow, her skin rosy, and her eyes glassy. But when her gaze travels downward and she sees how hard I am, her eyes grow sharp again.

"Do you want to fuck me, Liam?"

"Yes," I breathe. "Can I?"

Those perfect, pink lips curve upward into a smirk. "You'd better."

I quickly grab a condom from the nightstand and roll it over my length. One look tells me she's wet and waiting for me, so I line myself up with her entrance and slowly—so slowly—move my hips until I'm inside of her.

When I'm fully seated, I stay still for a moment. This is everything I've ever wanted and then some, and I want to appreciate it.

Lo's jaw goes slack as she squirms beneath me again. "More. Liam, please. I need more."

Her wish is my command. I set a slow pace, both of us falling into a rhythm together. Our gazes lock for a while until I can't stand it any longer. Our lips meet in a hot, messy kiss, our tongues the mirror image of our bodies coming together again and again.

Cupping her breast, I roll a nipple between my fingertips. She cries out, so I do it again. I can feel her walls fluttering around me, and I'm afraid I won't last much longer, so I thrust harder.

"Liam, yes. I'm so close."

"Come for me, Lo. Let me feel you."

And I must be the luckiest man in the world, because she does. Her pussy squeezes and releases around me, so tight that I have no choice but to come with her.

We stay joined together as we both come down from the high. I search her face for any sign of regret, but I only find a soft smile and a breathy laugh.

"We should have been doing that for years," she says quietly.

I draw her earlobe between my teeth. "I'm not opposed to making up for lost time. If you want," I add, searching her expression again.

She softens and runs her fingers through my hair. "I do," she says.

And my heart soars.

# Chapter 13

## Lo

"So you're telling me that your Grams has been sending you nutcrackers every year of your life including the years since she passed away." Liam is incredulous, and I can't blame him. It's weird as hell, and I still have so many questions about how she did it.

"Yes."

"And she's included notes telling you to check on the shop."

"Yes."

It's dark outside, and every once in a while, the wind will blow and send snowflakes drifting into the window. We didn't bother getting dressed—why would we when we find the desire over and over again to explore each other's bodies? Making up for lost time, indeed.

But now, Liam is laying on his back, one arm behind his head and one wrapped around me, keeping me close. My ear is pressed to his chest, and I can hear his heartbeat. Slow and steady.

"And when you went to the shop yesterday, there was another nutcracker there with a note for you."

"Yes. You can't tell me you didn't have anything to do with this." I shift so my chin is resting on his chest in order to see his face. "She clearly wanted me to come back here and find out you owned the place. She was hoping for a reconciliation."

"I swear to you, I didn't." His gaze drifts toward the ceiling as he thinks. "She obviously had a plan with that contract she gave me, though. It wouldn't be out of the question for her to have plotted out this whole thing and paid someone to send them each year until you came to your senses."

"Hey." I hit him lightly on the bicep, but he just laughs and squeezes me tighter.

"Do you want to know? It's a small town. I'm sure we can figure it out easily enough."

I chew on my lip for a moment, thinking. "Is it silly if I don't? It's weird, but it's *my* weird, you know? Pulling back the curtain would ruin the magic."

"I don't think that's silly," Liam says quietly, his voice full of sincerity. "It's Christmas. Magical things happen at Christmas."

Smiling brightly, I crawl the few inches up his chest to kiss him. That's when it hits me—this is home. Not Liam's house, exactly, though I could get used to living in the lap of custom-built luxury. But definitely Riverbend Springs with all its quirks and memories and people who love me.

But I don't know how I'd make it work. I have to go back to at least finish out the year. And Liam said the bookstore turns a very narrow profit each month. Would it be enough for me to live off of?

My indecision must be written on my face because Liam frowns. "You don't have to figure the rest out now."

"I know." I sigh, settling my cheek onto his chest again. "It's been a while since I've been this happy. There are just some loose ends."

He kisses the top of my head. "Sleep. Everything always looks different in the morning."

***

Nothing looks different in the morning. Liam makes excellent coffee and an omelet that might rival Jesse's holly jolly waffles. He kisses me at the door with promises to see me later, but there's no definite plan. And while I know he wants me to stay for Christmas, he told me all about his special Christmas Eve traditions with Mia. I don't want to impose on that, so I don't ask.

I have a lot to think about, so I don't mind being alone in Grams's house on Christmas Eve, but Mia wasn't wrong. It's kind of depressing without any decorations. My place—how did Grams put it? *That barebones, whitewashed city apartment*—was never decorated outside of the yearly nutcracker and a couple of things Natalia would put out. But that never seemed to matter because it was just me.

Now it's still just me, but I'm carrying all these memories, too. Grams's house was always full of Christmas cheer. We'd go cut down a tree at the local Christmas tree farm, and she had this little winter village she'd set up on the mantle. There was always something cooking, too. It smelled divine, whatever it was. Everyone was welcome on Christmas. Liam spent more than a few holidays here. I always thought it was because he needed a break from his family, but now I'm wondering if it was because he wanted to be with me.

I could leave teaching in the middle of the year. It's not impossible, though it could mean my teaching license would be suspended in Illinois for up to a year. But it would be wrong. My students would likely end up with a sub, and I'd be leaving Natalia in a lurch to find a new roommate, too. I have to go back, at least until May. That much is for sure.

The irony that I left this town—and Liam—all because I didn't want to try to have a long-distance relationship with him only to have to try a long-distance relationship with him over a decade later isn't lost on me. What a cruel joke.

Somehow, though, I don't think he'll mind.

As the sky darkens and the moonlight starts to glint off the new snow, I order a pizza, put on the all-Christmas radio station, and sit by the electric fireplace to feast. I haven't taken two bites before my phone rings. I jump up to answer it, excited that it might be Liam. But I'm equally excited to see Mom's name at the top of my screen.

"Hey, Mom."

"Hi, sweetie. Merry Christmas."

"Merry Christmas." My smile stretches wide as I hear the DJ call everyone who wants to do the limbo in the background. "How's your trip?"

"Good, good. Sunny, warm, the drinks are flowing... Are you home from Riverbend Springs?"

I hum lightly. "No, I'm actually staying here for the holiday. I'm in Grams's old house right now, believe it or not."

"Oh, good." She sounds relieved. "So it's still there?"

"Still here. Still exactly the same. Cleaner than it used to be, though." I can't help my curiosity. "Why?"

"Well, I was hoping you figured out your nutcracker situation, because I was just delivered an envelope with a letter from my mother with a deed to her house. It says here I can buy it for one dollar if I want to. Would you know anything about that?"

Shaking my head in disbelief, I laugh. "You want the short version or the long version?"

"Tell me everything."

So I do. The conversation twists and turns. We go off on tangents and share memories and laugh about stories from long ago. At one point, she leaves wherever she called me from and goes back to her room so it's quieter. We stay up well into the night, talking and laughing. But eventually, we both grow tired.

"You better go to sleep so Santa can come," Mom says.

"I don't know if he's coming here," I respond. "But that's okay. I found everything I want this Christmas, and then some."

"I'm so glad to hear it, sweetie."

"Do you think you'll buy the house?" I ask, looking around at all the pictures and knickknacks.

She sighs. "Probably. It'd be silly not to for that price." She grows quiet, then adds, "I miss it there."

"Yeah," I agree. "It's pretty great."

We say our goodbyes, and I click off the electric fireplace. I check my phone again to find a couple of messages from Liam that came in while Mom and I were talking. I send a quick response letting him know I'm headed to bed, hoping he's not one of those people who keeps his phone on all night so I don't wake him up. And then I tuck myself into bed and fall asleep.

# Chapter 14

## Lo

I'm rudely awoken by a very loud, very persistent banging. It takes me a few groggy minutes to figure out that the sound is coming from the front door. Begrudgingly, I roll out of bed, throw a hoodie on over the threadbare tank top and shorts I sleep in, and make my way across the house—on cold floors, like a peasant, I might add.

"Yeah, yeah," I mutter, wiping sleep from my eyes. "I'm coming."

The minute I throw open the door, a small human brushes past me. When I look down, there's a trail of glitter at my feet.

"Mia? What are you doing here?"

I can't see her, but her voice comes from the living room. "Decorating, of course. You can't have a Christmas feast without decorations!"

Blinking rapidly in confusion, I call back, "You can't have a Christmas feast without food, either."

"Yeah, we got that covered."

"Am I dreaming?" I ask as a gust of cold air blows in through the still-open doorway.

"Nope." Liam bounds up the steps with a two plastic boxes under his arm. He stops to bend down and kiss me. His lips are cold from the winter air. When he pulls back, I peek over his shoulder to see a Christmas tree poking out of the bed of his truck.

"What is happening?" I ask as I hug my hoodie closer around me.

Liam comes inside and deposits the boxes on the ground before heading back toward the door. "Mia insisted we bring Christmas to you this year."

"Your place is nicer," I call out to him as he hefts the tree out of the truck. I move further inside the house, both to make room for him to bring the tree in and because the cold air is starting to freeze my toes.

"Doesn't matter." He sets the tree down in the front room and finally shuts the door behind him. "You're here, so we're here." He kisses me again as if one day was too long without touching me. The whole house now smells like pine and snow, and Mia is singing an off-tune Christmas carol from the back of the next room.

"This is really nice," I say softly. Eyeing the boxes he brought in with him, I add, "There aren't any nutcrackers in there, right?"

Liam chuckles darkly. "I think there might be one or two."

"As long as none of them look like a wooden Father Christmas, I should be okay." I shudder. "I'm just going to change."

"Mia brought you an ugly Christmas sweater. It's our tradition."

He unzips his coat and, sure enough, he's wearing a red and green sweater that says *Sleigh-ing it!* over a picture of Santa in his sleigh. I don't think I've ever seen him in something so ridiculous, and it has me doubled over laughing.

"It's not that funny," he grumbles.

"On you, it is," I say between breathless giggles. I wipe my eyes just as Mia comes in the room, a bundle under one arm. Her sweater has a giant green tree on it and says, *Feeling pine!*

"We always wear ugly sweaters on Christmas," she tells me, handing over the one they got for me.

I take it from her and hold it to my chest. "Seriously, this is really nice of you both."

Liam makes a noise and winces. "Maybe look at the sweater before you get too sappy about it."

I unfold the fabric and, staring at me with a little smirk on its face, is a nutcracker. In big, bold letters on the top, it says, *Nutty or Nice?*

Mia is practically giddy, bouncing on her toes with her eyebrows raised. "Do you like it?"

I glance at Liam. His face is red from trying to hold back his laughter.

"It's...perfect for me," I tell her.

She jumps up and pumps her fist in the air. "Yes! Dad said you'd love it." And then she's off again, probably to sprinkle more glitter on the carpet.

"I really couldn't resist." Liam's voice is filled with laughter. I give him a playful shove, but he grabs my wrist and spins me to him. He holds me there, just gazing at me. "I don't know what this is to you or what your plans are, but I think we should probably keep Mia in the dark for now," he says.

"Of course." I check to be sure she's out of sight, then kiss him. "Makes sense."

"And when Tracy and Jesse get here...well...I didn't know what you wanted them to know."

"Wait, Tracy and Jesse are coming, too?"

Liam drags a hand through his hair, mussing it up even further. "I guess so? I called them for some advice and the whole thing kind of spiraled. The more, the merrier, right?"

That's what Grams always used to say about Christmas, and suddenly I'm emotional about it again. I just nod.

He lowers his voice so Mia can't hear. "I know you have to go back soon, and Tracy offered to take Mia with her tonight so we could talk. You don't have to decide anything right now, but I figured maybe it'd be good. But if you're not ready for that—"

I cut him off with a kiss that quickly turns heated. He moans quietly into my lips, and I drink it in, greedily. Before I'm ready, I pull away and give him a soft smile.

"That sounds perfect," I whisper.

"Okay." He brushes my nose with his. "Go change. Glitter Girl and I can take it from here."

"I heard that!" she calls.

"Oh, you heard that but not me telling you to brush your teeth this morning?" he shouts back.

"Fa la la la la—I can't hear you anymore!"

Shaking my head, I excuse myself to the bedroom, laughing all the way.

***

The decorations are nowhere near the winter wonderland Grams set up every year, but they're beautiful, nonetheless. Mia made most of them, and if Mom does buy this place, she's going to be finding glitter in crevices for the rest of her life.

Somehow, when she meets this kid, I doubt she'll mind.

Liam lifts Mia up high in the air to place the star he gave me at the Christmas Market on the top of the tree. She giggles the whole way. When we turn on the lights, she *ohhs* and claps her little hands with joy.

We spend most of the day playing board games. At one point, Mia gets so competitive, she tells me, "I'm going to win so hard that you're going to be the mayor of Loser Town." That's about when Liam shuts down the games and turns on a Christmas movie. Mia—who had apparently been awake at five sharp—falls asleep on the couch. Liam covers her with a blanket, and we use the opportunity to have a hot make out session in the bedroom.

Jesse and Tracy arrive with more food than anyone could possibly eat. There's a pot roast and vegetable platter and bread rolls. A lasagna appears from somewhere, too. Then, all the cookies and cakes and candy. Jesse even brings me some holly jolly waffles for dessert. It's messy and chaotic and loud.

It's perfect.

It almost feels like Grams is here with us, in this house that was always a welcoming place for me and my friends. And, as I take a minute away from some good-natured argument the rest of them are having about what Christmas song is better, I find myself gravitating toward the picture of her, Mom, and me in the front hallway.

As much as the nutcrackers freaked me out, I'm a little sad they'll most likely stop coming now.

But she was right. I had to come home in order to move forward. If I hadn't, I wouldn't be here, with a full belly, an even fuller heart, and a plan for my future that lights me up from the inside.

"Thanks, Grams," I whisper to her picture. And then I go to the bedroom to get something and return to the party.

"I have a present for you," I tell Liam as I hand him a shiny, wrapped box. Everyone grows quiet, turning their attention to us.

He frowns at me as I sit next to him. "I didn't get you anything."

I spread my arms, indicating our surroundings. "You got me all this."

Shooting me a skeptical look, he carefully slides the paper off the box and opens it up. Inside, there's a crisp, one dollar bill. He looks up at me, dark eyes brimming with hope and happiness.

Tracy and Jesse must know exactly what this means, because Jesse pumps his fist in victory, and Tracy makes a little squeal.

"Merry Christmas," I say, unable to resist my grin spreading from ear to ear. "I hope you like it."

"I love it." He looks down at the box, then back up at me. "Welcome home, Lo."

# Epilogue

## Lo

***One Year Later***

"Come on, Mia. We're going to be late!" Liam calls from the bedroom.

"I. Am. *Coming*!" she yells back. "I can't get this bow in my hair!"

I smooth a hand over my green velvet dress and take one last look at myself in the mirror. I look pretty damn good, if I do say so myself.

"I got it!" I yell. Somehow in the past year, Mia has become even more sassy, and Liam isn't quite sure what to do with it. I've stepped in as the mediator—and resident hair-braider. And I've never been happier.

It's December first, the day Liam and I picked to host the grand re-opening of The Nook. I wanted to do it on my birthday yesterday, but Liam insisted that the shop had a special connection to December, and so did Grams. He was right, of course, and so it was decided.

I went back to Illinois to finish out the school year, but the minute I felt comfortable putting in my resignation for next school year, I did. Every weekend—and some weeknights—I drove out to Riverbend Springs or Liam drove to me, sometimes with Mia and sometimes alone. We went on dates like a normal couple. We even took Mia to the city a handful of times. Then, late into the night, Liam would listen to all of my plans for the bookstore. Even later into the night, we'd share our dreams about our lives together and continue making up for lost time.

But it didn't take long for me to move back to Riverbend Springs. Mom did end up buying Grams's place, but she decided to use it as a retreat location for her ladies' group, so I couldn't live there. I talked about getting an apartment in Dubuque, but Liam wasn't having any of that. So, in June, I moved in with him. Mia was over the moon. Honestly, so was I.

For the bookstore re-opening tonight, Mia picked out a gold sequined dress with matching bow. Liam thinks she looks like a giant ornament. I think she looks perfect.

And when he comes in wearing a charcoal gray suit and a green tie to match my dress, I can't help myself. I kiss him deeply, unable to believe that he's finally mine.

"Gross," Mia whines when she sees us together.

"Interesting." Liam kisses me again. "It only makes me want to kiss her more."

We leave out the front door, and Mia immediately grabs Liam's hand for him to help her down the sidewalk to the driveway. Funny how she wants to be so independent, but she's still just a little girl who needs her daddy.

I take a quick look around the porch, half expecting to see a green box with a red ribbon waiting for me. But there's nothing there this year. And despite knowing there probably wouldn't be after Grams's mission to get me back to Riverbend Springs had been accomplished, I'm still a little disappointed.

"No nutcracker this year, huh?" Liam asks as I climb into the passenger seat.

I shake my head. "No. I expected it, I guess. But I miss her."

He reaches across the center console and takes my hand. "I miss her, too. But she's here with us today in her own way." He squeezes my hand in his. "She'd be so proud of everything you've done with the shop. And with your life."

I bring his hand to my lips and kiss his knuckles. "Yeah." I sigh. "Thanks."

When we get to the shop, there's already a crowd standing outside. Mom is here. So are Tracy and Jesse along with what looks like half the town.

A big, red ribbon is draped in front of the doorway, and a giant pair of scissors is leaning against the wall. I step up to grab the scissors, but Liam yells, "Speech!" and the crowd takes up the chant behind him.

"Okay!" I shout, laughing. The crowd quiets. "Okay. I don't have anything planned, so this will be short. But sixty years ago, this town came out for the grand opening of The Nook and Granny Bookstore. It was a different time then, and a different Gloria Carson standing here." The crowd laughs. "But through it all, Riverbend Springs has proven that community matters. You showed up for her, and you've shown up for me in so many ways." I scan the people, then lock eyes with Liam. "I'm proud to call Riverbend Springs my home, and I'm excited for you all to see the new Nook!"

With that, I open the scissors and cut the ribbon to cheers and applause.

Liam bounds up the small step to meet me. He squeezes me tight, then kisses my temple. "Just to warn you, Mia might have persuaded me to come decorate a little more last night." He winks. "You ready?"

"Hell yeah," I say, expecting to be greeted by her handmade decorations with tons of glitter. But when Liam opens the door, the first thing I see are the nutcrackers. They're everywhere—on tables and shelves, between books and on windowsills.

"Oh my god." Breathless laughter escapes me. "That's a lot of nutcrackers."

"Thirty-one," Liam says. "Every single one your Grams gave you over every year of your life."

"Oh," Mom cries as she comes through the door. She rushes past me, picking up the most classic-looking one. "She gave this to me in the hospital." Tears glisten in her eyes as she runs a finger gently over the delicate details painted on it.

"She gave that one to me when I was ten." I point at one that is playing the drums. "I went through a drumming phase."

"Glad that ended," Mom says under her breath.

"Which one did you get when you were six?" Mia asks. "I bet it was a good one."

"Oh, it was." I look around the shop until I find it on one of the bookshelves in the redesigned children's section. I pick it up and hand it to her.

"It's so glittery!" She beams. "I love it!"

Customers walk through the store, picking up books and admiring the changes we've made, but my family continues to look at each nutcracker as my mom, Liam, and I trade off telling stories about Grams.

Liam was right. She is here with us. In her own way.

"Hey, what about this one?" Tracy holds up a pink nutcracker that's carrying a stack of books.

I take it from her and turn it this way and that in my hands. "I've never seen this one before." I wave to get Liam's attention from across the room. He excuses himself from the conversation he was having and comes to my side.

"Did you add this guy to my collection?"

He frowns deeply. "I've never seen that one."

"You didn't put it out with the others last night?"

Shaking his head slowly, he lifts his gaze to mine. "You don't think...?"

"No," I say quickly. "Her job here is done. There's no way."

But later that night, as we're closing up the shop and I take one last, satisfied look around the place, my eye catches on that pink nutcracker, and I could swear it winks at me.

# Looking for another Christmas novella?

Will Beckett and Gemma's desire melt away after just one night, or will it snowball into something more? One thing's for sure—this Christmas, they might find themselves wrapped up in more than just holiday decorations.

*If you love grumpy/sunshine, adversaries to lovers, workplace romances where they get snowed in and swear it's "just for one night," you'll love this fun, quick burst of Christmas happiness this holiday season. Check out Christmas by Design today!*

# *Acknowledgements*

THE BEST PEOPLE AN author can surround herself with are those who don't bat an eye when she says, "Do you think I could write a quick novella?" And then, when she says, "Do you think I *should* write a quick novella," they say, "YES."

First and foremost, thank you to my husband for all the husband-type stuff, but also for never shooting down my ideas. You not only encourage me, you ensure I can do everything and anything I want. You're my favorite, my only, and my Christmas movie buddy. I wouldn't have it any other way.

Hannah, as always, you are an inspiration. I am so honored to continually have you in my corner.

To my PA, Kayla. Thank you for keeping me on track...and indulging me when I insist on getting off track.

A huge thank you to my early readers: Kayla, Kae, and Beth. Thanks for jumping in at the last minute and helping me make Lo and Liam's story the most fun it could be.

I can't forget to thank my street team. From help with promotion to moral support (and encouraging me to make my wildest stories into books), I couldn't do any of this without you. I am so grateful you're here to cheer me on.

A massive thank you to my agent, Katie Monson at SBR Media. Thank you for being in my corner every step of the way.

Jillian Liota of Blue Moon Creative Studio, thank you as always for a gorgeous cover! This one screams holiday magic, and I love it so much.

Thank you to my family and friends. To Jillian, Cait, Lexi, and Stefanie, thanks for supporting me, helping me outline and plot, and just being generally amazing people. To Julia, Sandy, Elizabeth, Jill, and so many others who have supported me from the start. To my mom, dad, brother, and sister-in-law who have been endlessly supportive for years. Dad, thanks especially for those nutcrackers.

And last but not least, thanks to you, dear reader. May your days be merry and bright.

# About the Author

Allie Samberts is a romance writer, book lover, and high school English teacher. She was voted funniest teacher of the year for 2023 and 2025 by her students, which is probably her highest honor to date. She is also a runner, and enjoys knitting and sewing. She lives in the Chicago suburbs with her husband, two kids, and dog. You can follow her on Instagram @alliesambertswrites, TikTok at @alliesamberts, sign up for her newsletter at alliesamberts.substack.com, and get other updates at www.alliesamberts.com.

# Also By Allie Samberts

**Leade Park**

The Write Place

The Write Time

The Write Choice

**Standalones**

Common Grounds

Love Out Loud

**Novellas**

Pumpkin to Talk About

Christmas by Design

Love in the Time of Conversation Hearts (with Hannah Bird)

A Holly Jolly Romance

**Coming 2026 from Page and Vine**

Not a Strong Enough Word

Not on the Same Page

Not the Way it Ends

*Stay up to date on new releases and grab some bonus content! Subscribe to Allie's newsletter at https://alliesamberts.substack.com*

www.ingramcontent.com/pod-product-compliance
Lightning Source LLC
Chambersburg PA
CBHW050423110726
47899CB00008B/2831